Longarm
hammer b
nutted dung beetles!

The man behind the rain barrel twisted around toward
Longarm, bringing both his pearl-gripped pistols to bear,
and snarling like a frenzied wildcat. Longarm's rifle barked.
The man popped off both his pistols into the dirt between
his spread black boots, and slammed his head back against
the rain barrel so hard that Longarm could hear the sharp
crack of his skull.

The man with the whiskey bottle out in the street
turned toward Longarm, dropped the bottle, and slapped
his hands to the two big Remingtons bristling on his
leather-clad thighs. He must have forgotten that he'd fired
the bottle's wick, however. He hadn't gotten either pistol
clear of its holster before the bottle exploded with a
whoosh as loud as a dragon's belch.

The bottle shattered, spraying the man from boots to
knees with burning whiskey.

Longarm held fire. No point in wasting a cartridge . . .

TABOR EVANS

LONGARM

AND THE
DOOMED BEAUTY

JOVE BOOKS, NEW YORK

THE BERKLEY PUBLISHING GROUP
Published by the Penguin Group
Penguin Group (USA) Inc.
375 Hudson Street, New York, New York 10014, USA
Penguin Group (Canada), 90 Eglinton Avenue East, Suite 700, Toronto, Ontario M4P 2Y3, Canada
(a division of Pearson Penguin Canada Inc.)
Penguin Books Ltd., 80 Strand, London WC2R 0RL, England
Penguin Group Ireland, 25 St. Stephen's Green, Dublin 2, Ireland (a division of Penguin Books Ltd.)
Penguin Group (Australia), 250 Camberwell Road, Camberwell, Victoria 3124, Australia
(a division of Pearson Australia Group Pty. Ltd.)
Penguin Books India Pvt. Ltd., 11 Community Centre, Panchsheel Park, New Delhi—110 017, India
Penguin Group (NZ), 67 Apollo Drive, Rosedale, Auckland 0632, New Zealand
(a division of Pearson New Zealand Ltd.)
Penguin Books (South Africa) (Pty.) Ltd., 24 Sturdee Avenue, Rosebank, Johannesburg 2196,
South Africa

Penguin Books Ltd., Registered Offices: 80 Strand, London WC2R 0RL, England

This is a work of fiction. Names, characters, places, and incidents either are the product of the author's imagination or are used fictitiously, and any resemblance to actual persons, living or dead, business establishments, events, or locales is entirely coincidental.

LONGARM AND THE DOOMED BEAUTY

A Jove Book / published by arrangement with the author

PRINTING HISTORY
Jove edition / December 2011

ISBN: 978-0-515-15018-6

JOVE®
Jove Books are published by The Berkley Publishing Group,
a division of Penguin Group (USA) Inc.,
375 Hudson Street, New York, New York 10014.
JOVE® is a registered trademark of Penguin Group (USA) Inc.
The "J" design is a trademark of Penguin Group (USA) Inc.

PRINTED IN THE UNITED STATES OF AMERICA

10   9   8   7   6   5   4   3   2   1

Chapter 1

Weary from travel, Deputy U.S. Marshal Custis P. Long, known to friend and foe far and wide as Longarm, tramped up the outside stairs of his second-story flat in a neat, frame rooming house on the poor side of Cherry Creek and froze in his boots. He stared down past the knob and lock plate of the green-painted pine door, his tired heart picking up a reluctant warning rhythm in his chest.

The half length of stove match he'd wedged between the door and the frame had fallen to the sill. It lay there on the painted oak, its red sulfur tip and ragged opposite end staring up at him in mute testament to surefire danger.

The federal lawman always wedged a matchstick in his door when he left his flat, so he'd know if anyone had come prowling around, possibly intending to lie in wait for him inside and gun him when he wandered in, weary from his latest assignment.

He'd given his landlady strict orders not to enter his flat when he was away. He did his own cleaning, which wouldn't be enough for some folks but was as much as he needed, since he was gone more often than he was home—his home essentially being the owlhoot trail—and he wasn't what anyone would call particular about such things, anyway.

He raised his eyes to the door panel two feet in front of him. His skin crawled with the half-conscious expectation of a sudden shotgun blast from within blowing a pumpkin-sized hole in the door and burrowing a similar hole through the dead center of his chest and painting the stair rail behind him with his own blood and shredded bits of his ticker.

Longarm swallowed.

He touched the end of his tongue to the underside of his upper lip, which was capped with a brushy, dark-brown mustache upswept in the longhorn style. Very slowly, he took one step back, wincing, hoping that his low-heeled cavalry stovepipes did not set a board of the staircase to squawking and giving him away—never mind that anyone inside likely would have heard him tramping with weary heaviness up the stairs only a few seconds ago . . .

Just as slowly, holding his breath, he let the saddlebags riding his left shoulder slide down to his elbow. From there, he lowered the bags soundlessly to the floor at his feet. In his right hand, he held his sheathed Winchester Model '73 repeating rifle on his right shoulder. Pressing his tongue harder against his upper lip, and sucking a short, silent breath, he lifted the rifle off his shoulder and leaned it against the rail to his right.

The carbine was too much gun for tight quarters.

Stepping back to the right side of the door frame, and out of the way of a possible blast from inside, he reached across his washboard-flat belly clad in a blue wool shirt and brown wool vest and unsnapped the keeper thong from over the hammer of the double-action Frontier model Colt .44 holstered for the cross draw on his left hip. He slipped the gun out of the holster, and held it at waist level, aimed at the door.

He'd just started to reach for the knob to see if the door was locked when a sudden *whoosh* rose from behind him. Pivoting, he gave a startled grunt and brought the Colt up, aiming over the rail and into the side yard of his landlady's house. The bird was a shadow rising amongst the poplars and maples and angling over the cinder-paved sidewalk and the sandstone street. It disappeared, but a moment later, from the direction the bird had flown, an owl cooed.

The hair along the back of the lawman's neck pricked.

An owl. The Injuns of most tribes said an owl heard at night was the darkest of omens.

"Shit," Longarm muttered, swinging back to the door.

He reached forward, slowly turned the knob. His heart fluttered when the knob kept turning. It wasn't locked.

Which meant someone was waiting for him inside.

Crouching and tensing, shifting his feet slightly, he continued to turn the knob. It clicked. The door fell slack in its frame and a one-inch gap shone between the frame and the door. The gap shone with flickering umber lamplight.

Not only was someone inside, but they were apparently making themselves to home. At a little after midnight, no less!

He sprang off his heels, hammered the door wide with his left shoulder. Throwing himself forward and down and hitting the floor on his belly, he heard the door slam against the wall with a bang. He looked up raising the Colt, which he held tight in his right fist.

His bed was just ahead to his right. There was something on the bed—round and covered in some thin fabric. Longarm blinked, frowned, raised his head farther.

A woman's bare ass stared down at him from the edge of the bed. Not quite bare but covered in just enough of a see-through shift to make the definition only slightly negligible. It wasn't covered nearly enough to hide the fact that it was a very nice, tight, round, pale ass tapering out wonderfully from slender hips. An ass that, at that moment, moved. The pink bottoms of two bare feet that also shone at the bed's edge but about four feet down from the ass moved, too.

Longarm looked around to make sure no one else

was in his small, shabbily furnished flat. Then he rose
up onto his knees and stared at the black-haired beauty
on the bed. She was just now twisting toward him and,
groaning groggily, lifting her head. She frowned, slit-
ting her cobalt-blue eyes framed by a delightful tangle
of long, straight, indigo hair.

Longarm's voice caught in his chest. "Cynthia?"

"Custis?" She sounded like she had a burr in her
throat. "What on . . . ?" She rolled onto her back and
propped herself on her elbows, blinking her eyes to
clear them as she looked from the kneeling lawman to
the door standing half open behind him. "What on
earth are you doing down there?"

Longarm lowered the pistol and rose from his knees,
blinking his eyes as if to clear them but glad that the
image of the naked young woman on the bed before
him did not go away. She wore the sheerest of sheer
black wraps—so sheer it appeared only a shadow spread
across her supple, curvaceous, full-breasted, trim-waisted,
round-hipped body. It came down to mid-thigh but did
nothing to hide the furred V between her legs.

"What on earth are *you* doin' up *there*?" he said
around the hard knot growing in his throat. "Tryin'
to give a man a heart stroke one way, and then . . .
another . . ."

Cynthia slid up in bed and, spreading her knees in-
nocently but giving Longarm a not very innocent look
at sundry private parts, fisted the sleep from her eyes
like a little girl awakened from her nap. "You're so late,
Custis. I thought you'd be here hours ago."

"How'd you know when I was getting in?"

"I stopped by the Federal Building and charmed the information out of that dapper little man in your boss's outer office."

"Ah, Henry." Longarm chuckled and dropped to his knees beside the bed. He wrapped his hands around the ankles of Denver's favorite debutante, Cynthia being a niece of the town's moneyed founding father, General William Larimer, and feasted his eyes on the girl's all-but-naked body displayed so richly before him. "Sorry about that. The train was held up by a wildfire between here and the Kansas line. Damn, how long you gonna be in town?"

"I'm leaving in the morning," she complained, pressing her rich lips into a delightful pout. "First thing."

She lowered her hands from her face and smiled suddenly, displaying all of those perfect, white teeth. Didn't rich folks ever get cavities?

"Custis, guess what?" She kicked her legs straight out and sandwiched his big, mustached face with strong, narrow hands. "A studio in New York City bought several of my watercolors as well as the oils I painted of you in the mountains—remember the ones, *sans* attire?—and they want me to bring them more! So I came back here to fetch the ones I've stored at Uncle William and Aunt May's, and I'm bringing them all back to New York with me for my very own personal showing!"

Longarm gulped. "You mean my pecker's gonna be on display in *New York City*?"

Cynthia tittered and pressed those incredible lips to his broad, sunburned nose. "Don't worry. I don't think anyone in New York City will recognize you. You're only famous west of the Mississippi. I think our secret"—she dropped her eyes toward his crotch—"is safe."

"At least, for now. Cynthia, what if someone who knows Uncle William and Aunt May buys those paintings you did of me in the raw, my pecker at half-mast because you were sitting there painting me in practically *nothing at all*—and they hang 'em somewhere dear Uncle William and precious Aunt May will *see* 'em?"

She stared at him. "I . . . guess I never thought of that. But not to worry, Custis. No one who knows anyone in my family is interested in my kind of art, I'm afraid. They buy only the staid and proper paintings, like those of Mr. Whistler and Mr. Sargent. They'd never dream of owning anything contemporary, and certainly nothing that depicts a brawny, naked man in the Colorado mountains with his big cock on full display!" She tugged on his ears, laughing. "Speaking of which . . ."

Longarm chuckled then, too, knowing she had a point. He ran his hands up and down her smooth, bare thighs and had to force himself to rise from the floor. "Hold on," he said, shrugging out of his brown frock coat dusted with coal ash from his recent train ride. "I'd best try to scrub some o' the travel grime off this old, tired carcass."

"Let me help you with that."

"Huh?"

She dropped her long legs over the side of the bed and rose, shaking her black hair back from her eyes. "You get out of those dirty clothes and lay down. I'm going to give you a sponge bath you'll remember on your deathbed."

Longarm watched as she turned her all-but-nude deliciousness away from him, and strode over to the washstand on which a cheap tin bowl and ewer sat. He had a bucket of water on the floor beside the stand, which he kept nearly filled for quick bathing purposes. As Cynthia bent over to pick up the bucket by its wire handle, giving him a view that would also be remembered on his deathbed, he felt a hard knot swell in his throat.

Humming to herself and casting him flirtatious looks over her shoulder, Cynthia poured water into the bowl. He jerked his string tie off, then lifted his blue wool shirt over his head; to hell with the buttons.

He tossed the shirt onto the floor, then kicked out of his low-heeled, mule-eared cavalry boots that fit his feet like old gloves. Standing, he shucked quickly out of his brown tweed trousers and balbriggans that had shrunk from so many washings that they fit his tall, brawny, sun-seared body like a second skin.

"My, my," Cynthia cooed as she carried the washbowl over to the bed, "you certainly are one fine hunk of a man, Custis Long."

"Yeah, you, too," he said, scuttling backward onto

the bed and resting his head and back against the plain wooden headboard.

She glanced at him, arching a brow.

"I mean," he said thickly, watching her heavy, pale, cherry-tipped breasts swaying around inside the black fishnet wrap, "you're . . . well, you know what I mean."

Cynthia gave a husky chuckle as she sat down on the edge of the bed and wrung a sponge out in the bowl, her eyes trailing across his left thigh to his full, engorged cock bobbing at full mast between the thick, dark tangle of hair between his legs. She leaned forward and touched her lips very gently to the tip of the iron-hard member, setting Apache war lances of pure pleasure rippling around under Longarm's hide, like worms under a log.

"Now," she said, straightening her back and running the sponge down over the top of his left thigh, "let's get you civilized, shall we?"

Her voice was deeply sexy and raspily alluring.

Longarm groaned as she worked, slowly bathing him as one would bathe a child—slowly, soothingly, cooing to him in an almost motherly tone and wringing out the sponge after every few caresses.

When she finished with his left leg, she washed his feet and worked her way up his right leg to his crotch. She gave his cock another slow, soft, but all-too-brief kiss, stoking the flames inside him once more, then, smiling beguilingly, she set to work bathing his arms and his belly.

Longarm lay back against the pillow, feeling every

muscle turn to butter. Every muscle, that was, except for the one that stood at full attention between his legs, waiting there, eager for more attention beyond the fleeting, teasing kisses from the beautiful woman crouching over him on the bed, her full breasts sloping toward him, a bud-like, tender nipple occasionally brushing his arm or leg or his belly or hip, silently enflaming him.

He reached up to cup one of those breasts.

"No," she chided him, pulling back slightly and brushing his hand away. "I'll do the touching. You just lay there and let me clean you."

"You're killing me."

She showed her fine, white teeth. "I know."

"Devil."

She chuckled again huskily, then gestured for him to turn over. Wetting the sponge, she dribbled water down his back, along his spine, then scrubbed every inch of his back and the back of his neck and behind his ears, and then his backside—even the bottoms of his feet. It must have taken her nearly a half hour, though to Longarm—with that hickory knot hardening in his throat—it seemed even longer. While her slow, damp caresses were infinitely soothing, his body hungered for her, his hard-on throbbing against the bed beneath him.

Finally, there was the soft plunk of the sponge being dropped into the bowl. She touched his shoulder, and he rolled over onto his back in time to see her rise from the bed and dump the water from the bowl into the chamber pot beside the night table.

Another nice view of her black snatch opening pinkly beneath the round, pale globe of her delightful bottom.

"Cynthia, Christ," he rasped, curling his toes in desperation.

"Just you wait, mister." She smiled at him over her shoulder as she splashed more water into the bowl. Then she returned to the bed, sat down on its edge once more, dipped the sponge in the bowl, and touched the sponge to the head of his hard-on. Longarm drew a short, quick breath. She ran the sponge down the iron-hard organ's underside to his balls.

He drew another fast, shallow breath.

She lowered her head, so her hair slithered across his thigh, tickling him, and touched her tongue to the underside of her upper lip as she slowly, deftly, torturously ran the sponge up and down and all around his throbbing dong.

Longarm's heart turned somersaults.

When she was finished, she returned the sponge to the bowl. She dumped the bowl out in the chamber pot and returned the bowl to the washstand. Longarm's cock was both hot from the blood coursing through it and cool and damp from the water Cynthia had washed it with. He lay there as though tied down, his heart thumping slowly now in his chest, distant bells of excruciating desire tolling in his ears.

"Now, then," Cynthia said.

She stood beside the bed, lifted the fishnet shift up and over her head, and let it fall to the floor at her feet.

Her hair fluttered like black feathers around her shoulders and the swollen globes of her breasts.

Longarm swallowed against the hard knot in his throat.

He stared up at her—his buxom, beguiling, cobalt-eyed executioner.

Slowly, she sank back down on the edge of the bed, crossed her fine legs, twisted her torso around and lowered her warm, soft breasts to his thighs. She wrapped both her hands around the base of his waiting member, and closed her hot, wet mouth of the swollen mushroom head.

"Oh, boy." Longarm flexed his toes and ground his shoulders into the sheets as she swallowed him. "Oh . . . oh, *boy* . . ."

Chapter 2

Longarm awoke at dawn, only an hour or so after she finally let him sleep, and only long enough to glimpse her dressing in the shadowy room, clothing that magnificent long-legged, round-hipped, full-bosomed body, tossing her long black hair.

The wind kicked up by her movements smelled like spring roses.

He'd drifted off for a time, exhausted from the long train ride from Kansas and the near-savage coupling with the delectable and tireless Miss Larimer—three times after her initial French lesson!—and was pulled up from his slumber once more when she kissed him lingeringly on the mouth, then giggled as she squeezed his already sore and chafed old member.

Just as the stalwart beast between his legs started to

come alive—like a grumpy, sleepy bear stirring instinctively to head back out on the hunt—she pecked his cheek, laughed raspily, nibbled his ear, told him she'd see him again in a month or two, when she returned from Paris or wherever the hell she was off to with her sketches of him in the buff, and left.

Her sketches of him in the buff . . .

"Cynthia!" he cried, jerking up in the bed and shooting his anxious gaze at the door.

He gulped. He was too late. She'd left when it was still almost dark, at least an hour ago. Now saffron sunlight filtered through the ash and maple trees that the city of Denver had planted along the street outside his boardinghouse on the poor side of Cherry Creek. Shadows were long. Dust motes filtered through the prisms of light angling through the soot-streaked door panes and the window over the small eating table at which he'd never actually sat down to a meal.

The indigo-haired she-tiger, portfolio of his naked pecker in hand, was probably heading into the far eastern reaches of Colorado now, maybe to Julesburg already, on her journey back to New York, where she'd display her sketches and oil paintings of him in the nude. She'd used him for a model last summer along the Arkansas River, up near the picturesque little mining town of Buena Vista, a two-day's train ride west of Denver. Somehow, she'd coaxed him out of every stitch of clothing, and now he, in all his nakedness, was on his way to the most populace city in the country—one of the largest in the world!

Oh, Lord—what if his boss, Billy Vail, learned that his most senior of federal law bringers was on full display in some highfalutin art gallery patronized by half the mucky-mucks on the East Coast? Or, worse yet, what if Cynthia's regal, legendary, filthy rich clan headed up by General William Larimer himself, and the kindly, pious, albeit perpetually befuddled Aunt May, found out he'd been exposing himself to his favorite debutante in the tall and rocky when Longarm was only supposed to have been the girl's unofficial *bodyguard*?

Two things settled the lawman down.

One—Cynthia had likely been correct when she'd asserted that no one who knew the Larimers, let alone Chief Billy Vail, would ever see the art in the first place, let alone recognize the burly, naked gent lounging in the verdant grass along the river, his big cock in repose across his thigh.

Two—the sun shining so brightly meant that Longarm was late for his nine o'clock meeting with said boss, Chief Vail!

Longarm glanced at the small clock hanging above his bed. Yep, he was late, all right. A whole five minutes already.

The big lawman shoved a wing of his dark brown hair back off his forehead, brushed a hand across his longhorn mustache that bore not one fleck of gray despite all his professional stresses and wild travails, and scrambled out of the bed still warm from the girl's supple, eager body. He dug around in his secondhand armoire for fresh clothes, duplicates of those he'd torn off last night in his haste to fuck the general's princess.

Then he scooped his saddlebags, saddle, rifle, and war sack off the top landing of the stairs outside his front door, and kicked his McClellan saddle through the open door and into his flat. He preferred the cavalry saddle to the bulkier western stockmen's saddle, but surely he wouldn't need it today. Billy wouldn't send him out of town on assignment the morning after he'd just returned from a three-week sojourn fighting back robbers out on the Kansas flats!

He knew that wasn't true, but he decided to risk it, for he was too tired from the journey, the fuck-tussle, and the abbreviated rest, to haul the heavy load up Colfax to the Federal Building.

Balancing the gear on both shoulders, he headed on down the steps. He'd walked only half a block before he begged a ride in the back of a coal dray to Colfax Avenue, where he leaped off under the burden of his gear and tramped past the U.S. Mint. It might have only been a few hours since he'd reveled between Cynthia Larimer's spread legs, but he grinned as he admired the female shop clerks and bank secretaries and hash throwers bustling to work in their lightweight summer frocks.

He dragged his gaze away from one such buxom, round-assed little lass, blond as the sun itself, noting that his obvious admiration for the girl was lifting a flush in her chubby cheeks, and hoofed it up the stone steps of the Federal Building.

He rushed through the heavy oak door under the

always-closed transom, said, "How's it hangin', Henry?" to the chief's snotty, dapper secretary.

The scrawny, little, bespectacled gent in a three-piece suit did not so much as glance over his shoulder at Longarm, nor slow his pace on the clattering keys of the newfangled typing machine, but merely wagged his head. Longarm dropped his gear on the floor, tossed his hat onto the elk antler rack to the right of the door, and headed toward the door flanking the young secretary's desk and on which CHIEF MARSHAL VAIL was stenciled in gold-leaf lettering.

A shadow appeared in the frosted glass of the door's upper panel. The door opened, and there stood the short, squat, balding, badly rumpled Chief Marshal Billy Vail, plucking a fat stogie from his wet lips and snarling, "Goddamnit, Custis, get the hell in here. You're late again. Twenty minutes late!"

"Ah, hell, Billy—!"

"Ah, hell, Billy—nothin'!" the Chief Marshal bellowed, sliding his eyes toward the clerk still busily—and now with a little self-satisfied grin—playing the typing machine's little round keys. "Henry, are Longarm's orders and travel vouchers ready?"

Without slowing his typing and keeping his eyes on the paper curling up from the machine's roller, Henry said smugly, "They've been ready for nigh on an hour, now, Marshal Vail. I have, in the meantime, gone on to other chores."

Longarm thought he saw the bespectacled secretary cut a sneering glance at him. As Vail gave an exasperated sigh and turned and strode back into his office and around his cluttered desk the size of a lumber dray, Longarm followed him in, suppressing the urge to stick his tongue out at the typewriting-playing dandy.

"I do apologize, Chief," Longarm said, "but, holy Christ—I just got back into town last night. *Late* last night!"

"I know when you got back into town. Somewhere south of midnight. But I done cabled you while you were still in Hays and told you I needed you in here by nine o'clock this morning and not a minute later!"

"Like I said, I'm sor—"

"You look like you been through the mill," Billy said, suddenly lowering his voice with concern. He sagged into his high-backed leather chair, letting his big belly push his wrinkled white cotton shirt and the top of his belted broadcloth trousers out to the edge of the desk.

"Yeah, well, it was a rough one," Longarm said as he dropped into the Moroccan red leather visitor's chair angled before Billy's desk. He sighed, flopped his arms. "One of the toughest assignments I been through in a long time. Wrote up some notes on the train ride back. I'll give 'em to Henry in a day or two."

"I would appreciate that," Billy said, "and cut the bullshit."

Longarm scowled. "Huh?"

"She was waitin' for you, wasn't she?"

"Waitin'? For me?" Longarm scowled with a little more effort. "Who'd that be, Billy?"

Billy leaned forward, jowls flushing, his washed-out blue eyes pinched to slits. "You know who I'm talkin' about. The Larimer girl. The big-titted, long-haired debutante you been fuckin' seven ways from sundown for the past two years against my dire warnings that, once the cat's out of the bag, the old general himself is gonna fill you so full of holes that the buckshot'll still be rattlin' around inside your casket when they drop ya under!"

Longarm let his scowl dissolve to a genuine expression of wonder. "You got a spy posted outside my boardinghouse, Billy?"

"Hah—I was right!"

"You mean—that was just a guess?" Longarm said indignantly.

Billy threw himself back in his chair and jiggled around like a delighted moron. "Yes, it was a guess. Wished I'd have bet money on it. Oh, you're a pistol, Custis. Just a goddamn pistol! I had a feelin' I still smelled the stud musk on you, saw that well-fucked look you always carry in here after you been dippin' your dick in that rich girl's honeypot!"

"Billy, you're a dirty old man. You ought not to be thinkin' about such things as what me and Miss Larimer do beneath the covers of a night." Longarm let a smile crawl across his broad, scarred, brown-eyed countenance. "Liable to give you a heart stroke, and I'd have to break in a whole new boss."

"In spite of what you may believe, it does not please me to think of you two together. You got no idea

the kind of trouble you're courtin'. My God, man—
you're a government employee. A wage earner. That
girl is *high fuckin' society*!"

"I don't intend to marry the girl—just screw her.
And, believe me, she wouldn't have it any other way."

Longarm laughed, dug one of his prized nickel che-
roots out of his shirt pocket, and stuck it between his
teeth as he fished a stove match out of his coat pocket.
His mind flashed to last night, and Cynthia lifting
both her bare legs over his right shoulder, to give
his ax-handle hard-on a change of angle as he thrust
it through the silky folds of her trembling, sopping
snatch.

He chuckled again.

"Talkin' to you's like talkin' to a brick wall," Billy
said, with a fateful wag of his head. He thumbed his
dirty, round spectacles up his nose, plucked a manila
file folder off an ungainly stack on the left side of his
desk, and tossed it over to Longarm. "No point in tryin'
to save your ass, I reckon. No time, neither. You're
train's gonna be pullin' out in a bout twenty-five minutes, so we'd best make this quick."

"I just want you to know I protest this out-of-town
assignment so close on the heels of my last one, Billy.
Even I need to rest up at least a day before I'm sent
back out on the wolf hunt."

"You could have slept last night. Instead, you chose
to fornicate like a back-alley cur."

"What would you have done—thrown her out?"
Longarm struck the stove match to life on his boot heel

and touched the flickering flame to the end of his cheap cheroot.

A tad sheepishly, knowing he was lying through his teeth, Billy said with the air of a Baptist preacher addressing his flock, "I would have told her, 'Thank you for coming, Miss Larimer, but perhaps we could set another time? I just got back from a long, tiresome journey, and my employer has ordered me into his office at nine o'clock sharp tomorrow morning—and I am far too dedicated to my job, my badge, and to the respected chief marshal himself to be even one minute late!' "

Longarm was choking so hard on his first smoke puff that he couldn't even laugh.

"Anyway," Billy said, scowling impatiently, "as I was sayin'—you got a train to catch! And this is serious business, Longarm, so I hope you have your brains in order after your love tussle. I need you more focused than ever for this job."

"What is it?" Longarm said, pounding his chest to work some fresh oxygen into his lungs, his face still flushed from the choking fit. "It best be important, dang it, Billy!"

"Matter of life and death, in fact," the chief marshal said, taking a quick puff off his fat, wet stogie and blowing a smoke ring over his crowded desk toward Longarm. "Death for one man—a hired Pinkerton bodyguard. Life for an important trial witness, if you can get to her in time."

Chapter 3

"You wanna chew that up a little finer?" Longarm asked his boss as he finally sucked a complete breath down his throat.

"It's all in the folder there. You can read it on the train. Just to give you some sense of where you're going and what you're riding into—remember that cousin of Cole Younger's, Little Babe Younger, who a local town marshal caught up in Snow Mound a few weeks back? The bastard was in the process of robbing a bank there, all by himself while he was waitin' for the rest of his gang, and the marshal somehow managed to throw a loop around him and took Younger into custody. Younger was no doubt drunk. Has a penchant for the firewater."

"All right—my memory's refreshed, Billy. This Younger worm break out of the hoosegow, did he?"

"Nope. He was held for trial there in Snow Mound. They were holding him on a charge of robbery only. But the town of Pinecone just west of Denver, near the base of Mount Rosalie, had a murder warrant out for the son of a bitch, for a previous bank job and murder. Well, the law bringers up thataway saw no reason to haul Younger down mountain to Pinecone and risk his gang springing him.

"So they sent a willing witness up from Pinecone to Snow Mound, to testify at Younger's trial that she watched from two feet away as the kill-crazy little rapscallion shot the Pinecone bank's vice president in the right eye from a distance of six inches. Blew the poor man's brains all over the bank vault gaping behind him. For no other reason than Younger didn't seem to care for the smell of the pomade with which the vice president oiled his hair."

"Okay, I'm with you so far, Billy. Younger got tried for murder up in Snow Mound. And the witness from Pinecone testified, did she?"

"Yes, she did. Very willingly, I might add. And Babe Younger was hanged all legal and proper for his murderous ways, on the main thoroughfare of Snow Mound, with a whole crowd gathered and clappin' their hands and hootin' and hollerin' and fireworks poppin' and kids and dogs runnin' wild."

"Typical small-town hangin', in other words." Longarm blew a smoke plume toward the banjo clock near the window in Billy's east wall. "So, what's the problem?"

"The witness is in trouble. Seems the gang got there too late to stop the hanging, but they're out for revenge. She's due to head back to Pinecone on the next train, only the next train is late due to a rockslide on the tracks. A crew of Denver and Rio Grande boys is working on clearing the rocks, but, in the meantime, the witness is stranded there in Snow Mound—with one of her bodyguards dead.

"She has one other man with her—apparently a Pinkerton hired by the president of the bank she works for in Pinecone. But there were two bodyguards at the start of the dance. Got a cable three days ago from the marshal up there in Snow Mound. One of the men he hired to protect the woman was shot by a sniper through the window of the café he was eating at—with the witness and the other bodyguard sitting across from him."

"Ouch."

"The killer didn't show himself, but the marshal's sure it's one of Younger's gang, which means the gang is likely hovering around the edges of Snow Mound, waiting for the witness to head to the train depot, once the narrow gauge arrives to haul her back to Pinecone. They warned her against testifying, and now that she has testified to great and irreversible detriment to one Babe Younger, Babe's friends aim to make her pay."

"You want me to go up and lend a hand with said witness, get her to the train on time," Longarm said, glancing at the banjo clock once more, then leaning forward to rub his cheroot out in Billy's overflowing ashtray. "All right, I ain't sure how this is a federal matter, but if you think it's so dang important . . ."

A little irritably, Billy said behind a cloud of roiling cigar smoke, "It's federal in a pinch because Younger had several federal warrants on his head. And you know how we always like to help out the local law bringers, Custis—especially when they're under siege by snarling trail wolves and cold-steel artists intent on mayhem. Most of whom are also wanted on federal warrants, I might add.

"The Younger gang's been pestering the mail trains for years now, but no one's been able to get close to 'em. Don't really even know who else is in the gang besides their now dearly departed leader, Babe his own vile self. They're a slippery bunch, holin' up in one damn mountain range or another up there above the clouds. It's rumored they have a main hideout over in Utah somewheres."

Longarm heaved himself out of his chair. "Two-, three-day trip up there, ain't it? The train has to wind way down through Pueblo and then through the Royal Gorge . . ."

"It's a long shot, you gettin' up there in time to help out. But I promised Webb Scobie—he's the marshal of Snow Mound and an' old friend of mine from my wild-'n'-wooly Texas Rangerin' days—I'd send a man to try to hold Younger's wolves at baby. And that's you. Oh, and one more thing," Billy added as Longarm turned to the door.

Longarm glanced back at his boss. A sneer cut its way across Billy's pudgy face.

"If you're thinkin' what I know you're thinking—that the female witness might be a real looker, and young, to boot—let me relieve you of your randy anticipation."

"Oh, don't tell me she's a crone, Billy!"

Chief Vail adjusted his glasses as he slid a telegraph flimsy before him on his desk, and said, "It appears here from Webb's missive that the woman you're looking for is one Mrs. Josephine Pritchard. Early fifties. Light gray hair, a tad on the portly side."

Billy snickered as he sat back in his chair and gave another little shiver of boyish delight.

"And sporting one wooden leg. The left one." He tapped his knuckles against the top of his desk. "Solid oak, I'd s'pect. Ha!"

"A wooden-legged old bat." Longarm scowled as he pointed his cold, half-smoked cheroot at the man giggling before him, through a heavy haze of churning gray smoke. "You're a son of a bitch, Billy!"

"Thank you." Billy's grin disappeared without a trace as he leaned forward in his hair, nailing Longarm with a commanding glare. "Now hurry on out of here. Your train's pullin' out in five minutes!"

"Hot-diggidy-ding-dang-dong!" exclaimed the honyocker sitting beside Longarm.

He ducked his head to see out the window of the

narrow-gauge passenger car's small, sooty window. The big, blocky chunk of rawboned man, who had informed Longarm after they'd boarded the Denver and Rio Grande at Union Station that he'd been a farmer in Dakota Territory until the snow and cold had driven him and his wife away, thumped the shoulder of the muslin-clad woman in the seat ahead of him. "Look at them canyon walls, Mother. Why, they appear to be climbin' all the way to heaven!"

The gray-haired woman in the crisp poke bonnet paused her needlework to look once more out the window. She shook her gray head and clucked, just as she'd done each of the half-dozen times that her husband, Hansel Anderson, had directed her attention outside over the past fifteen minutes, since the little train had choo-chooed its way into the mouth of the Royal Gorge.

"Those are some tall hills, indeed, Dad," the woman said in her thick Scandinavian brogue. "But Hansel, there is nothing on earth that could ever equal the glory of heaven!"

She glanced over her shoulder at her husband. As she smiled with satisfaction at her words, Longarm glimpsed the vibrant blue of her right eye beneath the brim of her cream bonnet marred by a few gray smudges of gray soot from the locomotive's smokestack and which dusted the hats and shoulders of nearly all the train's passengers. Esther Anderson blinked once, resolutely and serenely, then turned her head forward and resumed work on the little cap she was knitting for her new grandson.

The Andersons were on their way to live with their son, daughter-in-law, and newborn grandchild on a horse ranch in Nevada. Over the past six hours, Longarm had heard about the Andersons' plans and nearly their entire family history, until he'd considered taking his rifle, saddlebags, and war bag, and repairing to the roof of the pitching coach car for a little peace and quiet.

If there had been a saloon car, he'd have ridden there, his travel lubricated with Maryland rye and a distracting game of cards. But most of these mountain trains were fairly short combinations, as was this one, and there was nothing behind the chugging, smoke-spewing locomotive except a wood tender, two coach cars, a freighter, and caboose.

"Holy moly, though, Mother," intoned Hansel Anderson, nearly breaking his neck to peer up the twelve-hundred-foot, rocky, sunbaked northern ridge, "it may not be the stairway to heaven, but it's still dang impressive. Never seen nothin' like it before in my whole life!"

Anderson glanced at Longarm. "We don't have any hills even close to the size o' them ridges anywhere in Dakota, I tell you, Custis. Leastways, in no part o' Dakota I ever seen, and I lived there my whole life until just a few weeks ago."

The farmer and Longarm had been on a first-name basis for longer than the federal badge toter cared to think about.

"Oh, I reckon maybe the snowdrifts get almost that high, I reckon!" Anderson laughed at his joke and thumped his wife on the shoulder again. "Ain't that right, Mother?"

The old woman wagged her head agreeably and smiled down at her work. "Oh, Dad!" Anderson snorted raucously and laughed, sort of jumping up and down in his seat.

"Easy there, Anderson," Longarm urged. "This car ain't none too solid. You're liable to derail us, you keep jumpin' around like a chicken with its head cut off."

The big farmer, who had a nose the size and texture of an old ax handle, guffawed as though that were the funniest thing he'd ever heard.

Longarm excused himself, and went out to the rear platform for a smoke, where he enjoyed his hard-won solitude and watched the canyon walls slide by the train that was rolling along at about fifteen miles per hour, if that. They were moving so slowly along the gentle incline of the gorge's canyon floor that, he mused for lack of anything better to do, he could jump down on off the car, build himself a fishing pole out of string and an aspen stick, dig a worm out from under a rock, and snag a red-throated trout from the glistening waters of the Arkansas river sliding by, about ten feet from the railbed, and still hop the caboose before the train was out of reach.

He sat with his back against the coach's rear wall. He smoked, taking a few nips now and then from the hide-covered flask he carried in the pocket of his brown frock coat, his string tie buffeting in the wind. The Royal Gorge was a damn pretty sight with its sand-

stone walls, the river, and the cobalt-blue sky, the occasional hawk or eagle swooping over the sparkling water
whose headwaters were high in the deep mountains.

But Longarm had seen the gorge and the Arkansas
enough times that he now just wished there were an
easier, speedier route through the mountains directly
west of Denver. He'd heard rumors of a planned east-
west tunnel straight through the Continental Divide up
around James Peak, but until that colossal undertaking
had been met with a couple thousand tons of dynamite,
not to mention that amount of weight in brass balls and
human ingenuity, the southern dip down to Pueblo and
the slow, western plunge through the Royal Gorge
would be the only way to Colorado's central Rockies
and on to Utah and beyond.

The proposed tunnel, he'd heard, would cut the 340-
mile trip down to 180.

No one would have welcomed that cutoff more than
Longarm as, two days later, he stood on the same rear
platform, smoking and watching the sun-bathed, little
town of Dotsero slide into view along the east side of
the tracks. The town had been constructed at the con-
fluence of the Colorado and Eagle rivers, and it nestled
on a sage-stippled flat amidst high, snow-mantled peaks.

The winter hadn't been gone long from this high-
altitude oasis surrounded by gold and silver mines, and
most of the ridges wore their ermine, ragged-hemmed
gowns halfway down their bulky, granite slopes. The
white powder hadn't been gone from these lower pla-
teaus, either, for the sage and cedars were green as pol-

ished jade, with several creeks that fed the town still flashing cobalt blue. Most likely, they were tooth-crackingly cold.

His traveling gear mounted upon his shoulders, clutching his trusty Winchester '73 in his right hand, Longarm leaped down from the coach car even as it screeched and rattled to a halt before the rickety plank-board depot, plowed through rabbit brush and willows, and tramped down into the bed of a creek cutting up close to the gravel-paved railbed.

Longarm set his gear down.

It had been three days since he'd had a drink of fresh water. To numb himself against Hansel Anderson's innocuous conversation, he'd drunk too much rye, and his mouth tasted as though something dead had been putrefying in his throat for several weeks. Intending to rectify the situation straightaway, he got down on both knees, doffed his hat, and lowered his face to the spar-kling snowmelt stream.

The water was so cold that it instantly numbed his lips and tongue as, doglike, he lapped up the delicious brew that tasted refreshingly of snow and minerals.

"Hey, mister!" a man's voice called from behind him.

Longarm turned his head, water dripping from the ends of his longhorn mustache. He squinted up at a young man dressed in mismatched wool and wearing a soft, leather holster down low on his right thigh. The brim of his sun-faded bowler hat looked as though a whole passel of mice had been chomping on it. The kid stood atop the creek bank, feet spread a little more than shoulder width apart, thumbs hooked behind his cartridge belt, which glistened with fresh brass.

"Who's askin'?"

The kid spread a devious grin. "That's a good enough answer fer me!"

He'd just slapped leather and was about to bring up his long-barreled, walnut-handled Remington .44, when a boom as loud as detonated dynamite sounded nearby. For a split second, the blast seemed to suck all the air out of the world.

At the same time, the kid's head blew apart like a tomato obliterated from a fencepost by both bores of a double-barreled, ten-gauge shotgun.

Chapter 4

"You blew the demon's head clear off, Dad!" a woman trilled in jubilation from somewhere up along the tracks.

Longarm was still crouched beside the creek, staring in awe at the headless corpse standing before him, atop the creek bank. He'd been a lawman for a long time, and he'd fought in the war before that, but he'd never seen a sight as grisly as the one he witnessed now—the young man standing there before him, blood geysering up from his ragged neck to ooze down over the shoulders of his ratty, brown wool coat.

He stood sort of quivering, and for a moment Longarm thought he was going to break into a dance. His head had been vaporized by what Longarm assumed had been two barrels of large-caliber buckshot, and its hair, skin, brains, and bone fairly painted the ground around him. The kid still clutched his pistol, but now as Longarm watched, the young would-be shooter's hand opened. The pistol struck the ground with a thud. The kid's knees were buckling, and now they hit the weeds at the edge of the bank, and the lifeless, quivering, blood-oozing corpse rolled through the brush and down the bank, to pile up five feet in front of Longarm.

"Got him, Mother!" yelled Hansel Anderson.

Longarm saw the man running along the edge of the bank to stop at the top of the deer path that Longarm had followed down to the water. The Dakota farmer clad in blue-plaid shirt, suspenders, and knee-high, lace-up boots held a smoking shotgun low across his thighs as he grinned down at the man whose head he'd vaporized. Esther Anderson ran up to her man, lifting her gray skirts up above her blunt, black shoes, and clutched his arm as she, too, stared down at the farmer's handiwork.

"I reckon all that bird huntin' on the sloughs back in Dakota done honed your aim some, Dad!" She beamed. Then she narrowed one eye and lifted her pious gaze to Longarm. "A fork-tailed demon if we ever seen one. Dad here spied him first, Custis, as the would-be bushwhacker strolled so leisurely out of the depot house yonder and sauntered in your direction. Then I, too, saw him lift that hogleg from his holster, check the loads, and roll the cylinder like he expected to be usin' that little smoker real soon. Sure enough, he was."

She clamped a hand on the grinning farmer's big left shoulder. "The Lord's work is never done—eh, Dad?"

Longarm slowly heaved himself to his feet. He let his hand fall away from the walnut grips of his Colt Frontier .44-40, positioned for the cross draw on his left hip. He cast his gaze between the still-quivering corpse clad in blood-soaked brown wool to the two pioneers standing proudly above him, beaming as though looking out over a field of freshly harvested wheat.

"Holy shit," Longarm muttered, as several passengers from the train came over to see what the blast had been about.

"Such vulgarisms lack nobility, Custis," admonished Esther Anderson crisply. "And there is nothing holy in dung. Come, Dad—I'm tired and hungry, in need of food and rest before we make our next connection."

"You go on into the depot, Mother." The big farmer patted the middle-aged woman's hand. "I'll be along in a minute."

When the woman had gone, hefting two carpetbags and leaving the bulk of their luggage to "Dad," Longarm gathered up his gear and climbed the bank. He stood beside his coverall-clad benefactor as he glanced down at the dead man. "Thanks, Anderson." He squinted at the big double bore in the man's big, scarred hands. "You're right handy with that old popper."

"Shot a lot of geese back in Dakota. And any jaspers that tried to crowd me. You'd best watch yourself, Custis. If this man here was out to blow your wick, there could be more."

"I do believe you're right," Longarm said, as the big farmer clapped him on the back and, setting his shotgun on his shoulder, headed off toward where his and "Mother's" luggage was piled on the platform flanking the depot building.

Several men from the train milled around Longarm, smoking and glancing down with looks of revulsion at the dead kid lying near the cold creek, and at the bloody, boney spot in the sage and fescue near Longarm's boots, which was all that remained of the would-be killer's head. All the men appeared seasoned frontiersman, but one had to gulp to keep his lunch down as he turned and walked away, fatefully shaking his head.

Longarm saw a short, potbellied, bandy-legged man in his mid- to late fifties walk out the depot building's rear door, under a large rack of elk antlers, and look around, squinting beneath his high-crowned Stetson. When the man saw Longarm standing on the bank of the creek, he waddled over, scowling inside his patchy gray beard and fingering the big pistol wedged behind his wide, brown belt.

"What the hell's all the commotion out here?" he said in a deep, raspy voice. He wore a soiled white shirt under a dark-blue vest and corduroy coat. Green duck trousers billowed out around his short, bowed legs to disappear into his high-topped, mule-eared boots. "Sounded like thunder, but when I come out of Murphy's saloon, it was clear as a spring Sabbath." He gasped when he followed Longarm's gaze to the headless corpse. "Good Lord, man! What goes on here?"

"You the law here in Dotsero?"

"Constable Pete Jenkins—that's right. Now, I'll thank

you to answer my question. I try to keep a quiet town, though it ain't easy of late, with all you troublemakers blowin' through, heading for the diggin's higher up! Good Lord, man—where's his head?"

"Right over there, Constable. It's the gooey stuff in the grass. And I do apologize for the mess. My name is Custis Long, Deputy Unites States Marshal out of Denver. Any chance you recognize that headless younker down there, although I'll admit it would be a tad easier if he wasn't missing his face."

The oldster made a sour look as he stared down at the now still and silent dead man. "Can't say as I do. Oh, I seen him around town earlier, but I never got his name. Rode in last night. Stabled his horse at Greeley's Federated. Holed up at Miss Madigan's place. I take note of all strangers, and it ain't hard. Dotsero only claims about fifty reg'lar inhabitants, so strangers stick out like canker sores on purty whores."

"Did you happen to see which way he rode in from last night?"

"I did. He came down along the Colorado River from the north."

"That wouldn't be the direction of Snow Mound, by any chance?"

"It would, indeed."

Longarm fingered the trigger of the Winchester he was resting on his shoulder, peering north, where he could see the Colorado cutting down through a broad canyon sheathed in pine-covered slopes. He looked at the local badge toter, who stood with his hands in his pockets, jingling change as he pondered the dead man.

"Has the rail line been cleared between here and Snow Mound yet, Jenkins?"

The constable shook his head. "It's been cleared, but they're repairing track. Up on that high pass, it takes a while. The last cable we got from Snow Mound said the line wouldn't be open for several days, yet." He pointed at the headless corpse. "Who shot that feller? I don't see a gun on you big enough to have blown his punkin clean off his shoulders like that!"

Longarm didn't want the Andersons held up by local red tape, especially after Hansel had gone to the trouble of saving his life. "Just a passing benefactor, Jenkins," Longarm said with a grin. "Didn't catch his name. Long gone, now. You'll probably find enough jingle in the kid's pockets to have him properly buried." He shifted his gear on his shoulders. "His horse is over at the Federated, you say?"

The lawman nodded. "It's right next door to the James Peak Saloon."

"How far is it by horse to Snow Mound, Mr. Jenkins?" Longarm asked as he headed toward the depot house.

"It'll take you a good day. Say, this ain't anything about that lady who went up there to testify against that Younger jasper, is it?"

"What part of it?"

"Hell, all of it!" the lawman intoned with exasperation.

"I don't know," Longarm said as he ducked through the station house door. "I'll let you know on my way back through your quiet little town."

Longarm hadn't merely been being coy with Constable Jenkins. He really did not know if the dead younker's attempt at cleaning Longarm's clock had had anything to do with the Younger gang.

Longarm had plenty of enemies, and the kid might have been one of them. Spying Longarm hop down from the train, the kid might have decided to take this opportunity to burn him down for having had his pa or brother or maybe a cousin hauled away to a federal pen or a gallows.

On the other hand, the gang holed up around Snow Mound, waiting to perforate the stringy old hide of the wooden-legged Josephine Pritchard for testifying against their fearless leader and thus causing him to stretch hemp on the main street of Snow Mound, could very easily have learned that a federal lawman had been sent for.

The gang might have sent the kid down to waylay him with a bullet to his ticker. That's likely what would have happened, too, if Hansel Anderson hadn't been there with his barn blaster. Longarm chuckled at his bacon having been saved by a hooplehead from Dakota Territory, though he felt a chill at the back of his neck, as well—close one!—as he tramped on out the front door of the depot building.

He angled toward the right side of the broad street facing him. The high-altitude sun reflected off the finely churned dust and horse shit and the dusty shop windows, and smacked his face like a splash of warm tequila thrown by a truculent sporting girl. There were only about five or six false-fronted business establishments on either side of the street, with cabins hunkering in the sage and cedars behind the shops.

Stock pens and chicken coops sent up their expected aromas, as did a burning rubbish pile behind a hardware store. Somewhere, a rooster crowed and there were the intermittent brays of a typically cantankerous mule, probably voicing its irritation at a wind-blown tumbleweed or some such.

Longarm found Greeley's Federated Feed and Livery Barn. He saw no point in renting a horse when the young man who'd tried to perforate his hide had so recently orphaned a broad-barreled, stout-legged blue roan with clear eyes, good teeth, and four shod hooves in good repair. The horse looked mountain bred, judging by the thickness of its cannons and the heavy muscling of its haunches, and could handle the thin air of the rugged ride up to Snow Mound, which, the liveryman informed Longarm, was nearly ten thousand feet above sea level.

Longarm's federal marshal's badge was all he needed to spring the roan. The liveryman informed him of a shortcut trail to Snow Mound, one that was steep but would cut at least one hour off the usual route that followed the narrow-gauge rails along a switchbacking, time-consuming trace graded for the trains as well as wagons. Bidding the liveryman good day, the lawman led the saddled horse out of the barn, slid his Winchester into the dead kid's saddle boot, and stepped into the saddle.

It was nearly three o'clock in the afternoon. The western ridges were pocking with purple shadows beneath the low-angling sun, but he'd get a few hours' ride in, just the same. He'd hole up along the trail overnight, and get an early start the next morning. According to Mr. Greeley, that should bring him into Snow Mound around ten a.m.

He picked up the trail along the Colorado River that was a roiling tumult this time of year. He felt the spray from a near rapids as he put the big roan up a steep hill, and it was as cold as stardust. The water roared and chugged and dug up rocks from its bed and threw them, flinging chunks of driftwood this way and that. Longarm followed the trail off away from the stream and climbed through aromatic woods, following a switchbacking trail through fragrant spruce and balsam that offered welcome shade from the hammering, high-altitude sun.

He crested the ridge and rode out into a lush meadow perfumed by columbine and bright with wildflowers of all colors and designs. An hour later, he crossed a windy pass still crusted with snow patches that were littered with pine needles and cones and squirrel and rabbit shit. It was cold up here, though the sun still threatened to sear through several layers of skin despite his hat. He was glad to get back down the pass's other side and into a sheltering forest of aspens that were fresh smelling and vibrantly jade with new green.

As he rode through the trees, following the faint horse trace that was likely an old Indian hunting trail and which he occasionally lost sight of amidst new growth or deep forest duff, he kept an eye skinned on the terrain all around him. There was no telling when another grinning killer would try to drill him with an unwanted third eye, to keep him out of Snow Mound.

If that was the first would-be assassin's intention, that was. He thought it was.

When the sun had been down behind the forested western ridges at least an hour, he stopped and set up camp in an old burn amidst fire-blackened lodge-pole trunks. The fire had occurred a few years ago; new growth had sprung up in the form of shrubs and fetlock-high grass though here and there the blackened ash could still be seen, making the ground spongy. The dead trees offered seasoned wood for burning.

After Longarm had tended the big blue roan and spread his gear in a hollow amongst the skeleton-like trunks, he started a fire. It was getting cold, and he donned the heavy buckskin coat he'd wrapped around his bedroll. In spite of the fire, his breath frosted in the fast-darkening air around him.

To the north of his campsite, a rock wall offered cover. To the south, and down a gentle incline, lay a narrow valley through which a creek gurgled along the base of a steep, fir-carpeted ridge. The early night was so quiet that the creek sounded like chimes. Occasionally, a squirrel chattered, and chipmunks scuttled, striped tails arched, through the grass.

Later, Longarm had finished a spare supper of jerky and hardtack and was sitting back against a log, sipping coffee laced with rye, when his muscles tensed suddenly. He looked around. Men's distance-muffled voices rose from out in the thick, chilly darkness, down the incline and near the creek.

The big roan whinnied shrilly, pricking the hair under Longarm's collar. Instantly, his Winchester was in his hands, and he was cocking it and rolling away from the fire.

Chapter 5

Longarm rose to his haunches just beyond the pulsing sphere of light from his cook fire. He waited, expecting a gunshot.

He listened, his keen ears picking out every sound in the hushed mountain night—the crackling of his own fire to his left and which was sending up glowing cinders toward the blackened bows overhead. The tinny murmur of the stream down the grade ahead of him. The occasional, soft thud of a cone tumbling from a living pine, and the brief, fleeting rustle of an almost imperceptible breeze.

Very slowly, he straightened. Quietly, he racked a cartridge into his Winchester's breech and moved up to a charred tree bole straight ahead of him, pressing a shoulder to the scorched, barkless tree while staring off to his right, waiting to see if the rasp of his cocking lever would draw gunfire.

Nothing.

Longarm stepped out from around the tree and strode slowly down the incline, his jaws and his back drawn taut with tension. He set each boot down carefully, not liking the unavoidable crunching of the deep ash beneath the layer of new grass and pine needles. Weaving around the trees, he stopped after he'd walked about seventy yards.

From here he could see the flashing of the stream along the base of the steep ridge. Amidst the water's trickling and gurgling, he heard a branch that had likely gotten hung up in a riffle and was scraping against a rock.

He stood pressing the brass butt plate of his Winchester against his right hip, gloved thumb caressing the cocked hammer. Had men passed this way? He could see no signs of horses, though the night was so dark they'd be hard to pick out. On the other hand, the voices might have come from the opposite ridge. The incline there was too steep for horses, but not too steep for men working their way down from the ridge crest, intending to steal up on Longarm's camp.

He glanced over his shoulder to look back up the slope. His fire made a low, flickering glow in the darkness, not much brighter than a lamp from this distance and vantage.

A sound from across the creek made him swing his head forward again. A rock or something tumbled down the ridge and plopped into the water. Directly across from Longarm, two copper lights no bigger than his thumbnails glowed with primal menace. A cat's shrill cry assaulted his ears.

He stumbled back with a start, raising his Winchester. As his eyes lowered and he could see the silhouette of the cat's square head with the triangular ears sticking up—the wildcat appeared to be crouching, preparing for a leap from the ridge—Longarm squeezed the rifle's trigger.

The gun's roar slashed across the silent night, drowning out the stream. At the same time, Longarm's right boot heel rolled over a rock. The lawman lost his balance. He tore his left hand from the rifle, throwing it out for balance a half second before his ass hit the ground hard, cracking a branch. He grunted against the jarring reaching up through his hip and prickling his ribs.

Quickly, sitting there on the soft earth with the branch prodding his rump, he spread his legs slightly, lifting his knees, and levered a fresh round into the Winchester's breech. He raised the rifle to his shoulder and aimed at the spot between rocks where he'd seen the glowing copper eyes.

They were gone.

More stones tumbled down the ridge to plop into the water. He glimpsed a shadow moving out from behind a rock farther up the ridge and to his left, and then there was the crack of a branch snapping, and the shadow, too, was gone.

Again, except for the stream's murmur, silence.

Longarm ejected the hot shell from the Winchester's breech, saw it flash in the starlight as it arced out over his left shoulder to hit the ground with a soft snick, then racked a fresh round and waited.

Had it been the hunting cat's mewling he'd heard, mistaking it for men's voices? He could have sworn that what he'd heard had been human murmurings, but it might have only been his imagination playing tricks on him. He knew from experience that nights in the mountains were weird times. The air was so light and dry that you'd swear you could hear the stars crackling overhead, from billions of miles away. The trickling of the river could build in a man's imagination until it wasn't moving water at all but a whole cavvy of rampaging Utes.

Longarm heaved himself to his feet. He looked around and listened for another five minutes. When he heard nothing more but that which he'd heard before, in addition to a wolf expressing his loneliness from a faraway ridge to the north, he dropped down and took a long drink from the stream.

The water was so cold he thought his molars would splinter, but it tasted good and refreshing. When he'd had his fill, he shouldered the Winchester, tramped back up the incline to where his fire had burned down to a low glow, poured a fresh cup of coffee, and laced it from his bottle of Maryland rye.

He left the fire low, and sat away from it for a time, sipping his coffee and whiskey and staring out across the starry valley. The wolf continued to howl, stopped, and then two from separate ridges resumed the dirge.

The night settled cold as a Dakota winter, the coffee smoking like a wildfire in Longarm's hands. Finally, he threw back the last of the bracing, satisfying brew, and relieved his bladder, his pee steaming amongst the pine needles.

He set his cup on a rock, built up his fire from the dry wood he'd gathered, and pulled his saddle and bedroll up close to the flames. He figured it was down around forty degrees or so. It would get down below freezing by midnight.

He removed his gun belt, coiled it around his holster, and set the rig within easy reach beside his saddle. He leaned his cocked Winchester nearby, then dug a hole under him for his hip, rolled up in his blankets, enjoying the heat of the snapping, crackling blaze. Folding his arms on his chest and rolling onto one hip, facing away from the fire, he willed himself into a shallow but badly needed sleep.

He started hearing rifle fire late the next morning, as he climbed a slope through blowdown spruce and aspen, heading toward a sun-splashed saddleback ridge. The pops and cracks were too distant for the shooting to be meant for him, but he reined the roan to a halt, just the same, and slipped his rifle from the saddle boot.

The shots were muffled by distance and seemed to be rising from the other side of the ridge looming ahead and above him. He cocked the Winchester, set the hammer to half cock, and rested the rifle across his saddlebows as he batted his heels against the roan's flanks, and the big horse lunged off its rear hooves.

The sporadic fire continued as Longarm and the stalwart horse climbed the ridge along the narrow trail slanting through stands of stunted spruce and Douglas fir. Near the crest, Longarm dismounted, grabbed his field glasses out of his saddlebags, ground-reined the roan, and tramped to the crest, negotiating a talus slide still patched with dirty winter snow.

He hunkered down behind a boulder. Up here, the cold wind bit him, threatened to rip his hat from his head. He raised his coat collar, pulled his hat down tighter, and peered down the other side of the ridge.

Snow Mound sat in a roughly triangular valley below him. It wasn't much of a town, but he could see several large stores—probably hardware shops or mining suppliers and saloons—and the narrow-gauge railroad crawling into the valley from a canyon mouth to Longarm's left. Near the tracks were stock pens, a large, wooden water tower on stilts, and several mountains of split firewood.

The town was set at an angle before him. In the bright, cool sunlight, he could see the smoke puffs of blasting rifles or pistols around one of the large buildings on the other side of the main street from him. Answering shots sounded from a large, three-story, white-frame structure on the side of the street nearest Longarm.

The cracks and pops of the gunfire reached Longarm's ears about half a second after each smoke puff. Men's shouts rose, as well. Aside from the shooters, Longarm saw no other movement anywhere in the town, as though the place were under siege and all citizens were cowering inside their hovels.

He rose from behind the boulder and ran across the slippery, clacking talus to the roan, gathered up the reins, stepped into the saddle, and urged the horse up and over the ridge and down the side facing the town. Halfway to the bottom of the slope that dropped toward the shaggy northeastern fringe of the village, he swung the roan left, continuing on down the steep hill but now heading toward the settlement's other side.

Instinct told him that the instigators of the gun battle were those shooting from the far side of the main street. He intended to work around behind them.

He was glad he hadn't misjudged the roan. The horse was as good at moving down a steep slope as it was at climbing one, picking its footing carefully but able to continue moving quickly, leaning deep on its stout forequarters and stumbling little.

Leaping occasional slash and weaving around stunt pine and shrubs, the horse gained the bottom of the slope, leaped a narrow creek, and galloped around to the town's southern end, in the direction of the narrow-gauge rails and depot building.

Still, Longarm saw no one except the shooters out and about. Obviously, the shacks weren't abandoned, as smoke twisted from chimney pipes and horses and other stock milled in pens and corrals.

Longarm urged the horse around privies and pens and finally pulled up near the rear of the large, unpainted frame building he'd figured to be a saloon and from the front of which the brunt of the gunfire issued, echoing around the near ridges. Behind a two-hole privy, he leaped down from the roan's back. As he made his way toward the main drag, he saw three brightly dressed and feathered girls crouching behind the unpainted building fronting the privy.

A man stood near the girls—a short gent in a pinstriped shirt, sleeve garters, and a green apron. He was casually smoking a cigar while the girls crouched anxiously, one sneaking a look around the rear of the building toward the front, where the guns were popping.

Longarm approached the group. The man narrowed a skeptical gaze at him, puffing smoke around his stogie. One of the girls turned toward Longarm, then gasped and fell back against the building with a start. The other girls saw him, then, too, and they nearly leaped out of their high-heeled shoes and low-cut gowns and corsets as they cast fearful gazes at the imposing figure in the snuff-brown hat and three-piece suit, and holding the Winchester on his shoulder.

Longarm touched two fingers to his mustached mouth, and dug his moon-and-star federal badge out of his vest pocket, holding it up for all to see. Keeping his voice low, he said, "Who's flingin' lead at who?"

The man, who was obviously the bartender of the saloon behind which he and the girls had taken refuge from the dustup, removed the stogie from his mouth, and said, "Younger's boys are flingin' lead at the hotel and that Pritchard gal and Marshal Scobie."

"Figured as much," Longarm said as he pinned his badge on his vest. "How long the lead been flyin'?"

"'Bout a half hour. Haven't heard much shootin' from the hotel, though. Might be that old Scobie finally bought it." The barman scowled in disgust. "I told 'em they shouldn't hold the trial up here. Not without enough lawmen to keep that girl from gettin' perforated." His scowl deepened. "Where the hell you been? I hope you ain't *alone*!"

"How many of the Younger gang are out there?"

"Just three," said one of the girls—a pale, green-eyed redhead. She looked scared as she huddled low against the saloon's rear wall. "But there's plenty more where they came from just down the canyon at Miss Barbara's place."

"Just three, huh?"

"Three of the worst of Babe's whole gang," warned the barman, grumpily puffing his stogie. "Damn near wrecked my place this mornin', before they started pepperin' the hotel with their pistols and rifles and howlin' like banshees, scarin' the whole damn town into heart strokes! Me—I been to the dance before. But the hoopleheads around here like things *quiet*!"

"Yeah—me, too." Longarm lowered his rifle and peered around the saloon toward the main street. "You all just stay here, mum as church mice. I'll go see if I can't quiet things down a bit."

He stole out from behind the saloon and headed through the break between the saloon and another building toward the thundering guns at the front.

Chapter 6

As Longarm made his way up along the saloon's east wall, a man shouted from ahead, directing his voice toward the hotel on the other side of the main thoroughfare.

"Hey, Scobie. I got me a feelin' you're outta bullets, old fella!" The man gave a wild, coyote howl. "You wanna throw that little bitch outta there now, and save your stringy, old hide? Or, how 'bout me an' Willis and A. W. here burn the Snow Mound Inn right down to the street—you an' the girl along with it?"

The gunfire had died suddenly.

Now, halfway up the saloon's rough wooden wall, he stopped. Ahead, near a hitchrack, a man knelt behind a rain barrel, two smoking pistols in his brown hands. He was peering over the top of the rain barrel toward the hotel, the front of which Longarm could now see from his position. A man in a gray wool suit lay on the boardwalk fronting the Snow Mound Inn, belly down, one arm hanging off the boardwalk into the street. A bowler hat lay nearby. Blood glistened on the back of his coat.

Another man stood to the left of the rain barrel, sauntering into the street. He held a bottle of whiskey in one hand, a burning hunk of stove wood in the other. A long strip of cloth dangled from the mouth of his whiskey bottle. He wore two pistols from holsters thonged low on his thighs.

"Scobie—you hear me in there, old man?" he shouted, tipping his head back. A felt sombrero dangled from a thong down his back. He laughed and touched the burning stick to the wick dangling from the whiskey bottle.

Longarm stepped forward, thumbing the Winchester's hammer back to full cock. "Hold it there, you mushy-nutted dung beetles!"

The man behind the rain barrel twisted around toward Longarm, bringing both his pearl-gripped pistols to bear and snarling like a frenzied wildcat. Longarm's rifle barked. The man popped off both his pistols into the dirt between his spread, black boots, and slammed his head back against the rain barrel so hard that Longarm could hear the sharp crack of his skull.

As the man with the whiskey bottle standing half-way out in the street turned toward Longarm, he dropped the bottle at his feet and slapped his hands to the two big Remingtons bristling on his leather-clad thighs. He must have forgotten that he'd fired the bottle's wick, however. He hadn't gotten either pistol clear of its holster before the bottle exploded with a *whoosh* as loud as a dragon's belch.

The bottle shattered, spraying the man from boots to knees with burning whiskey.

Longarm held fire. No point in wasting a cartridge.

As the flames leaped up around his legs, the man in the street screamed and dropped his guns and hopped around, brushing at the flames as though to douse them. The wild movement only fanned the hellish fire, however.

The outlaw's frantic cries grew louder and shriller. Then, when he saw that his dancing wasn't working, he suddenly twisted around and started running eastward along the street for no understandable reason than maybe the creek was out there. The cold water was too far away. The man blazed past Longarm like an earthly comet until, a block away, he crumpled to the ground and lay still but for the helpless flopping of his arms and legs.

Longarm swung his head back toward the front of the saloon, hearing the thuds of running footsteps. He ran up onto the boardwalk fronting the big, glass windows and batwing doors and gained the boardwalk's other end in time to see the third gunman run around behind a feed barn about seventy yards behind the saloon, near the narrow-gauge rails. Longarm started after him, then stopped. The man reappeared on a big, gray horse, galloping off away from the barn and corral, flopping his arms like wings and glancing warily over his right shoulder.

Longarm cursed, dropped to a knee, and raised his Winchester. The man was moving too quickly away in herky-jerky fashion for accurate shooting, but Longarm triggered a shot anyway. And watched the slug puff dust far wide and behind the retreating rider galloping toward the far, southern ridge.

The lawman cursed again and walked back to the front of the saloon. The man he'd shot lay slumped on one shoulder, his eyes half open and glazed in death, blood dribbling in several rivers down his forehead and pumping out from the ragged hole in his chest.

The other man had burned down to the size of a modest trash fire. A big collie dog had appeared in the street nearby, tracing a broad circle around the burning man and whining with its head down.

Longarm turned toward the large, white hotel directly across the street from the saloon. The front door was closed, but its window as well as the rest of the glass in the building's façade had been blown out. Only ragged shards remained. Most of the windows in the two upper stories had also been blown away, their curtains hanging in tatters.

The man in the gray suit lay slumped and unmoving on the boardwalk fronting the place. A breeze had come up, however, and blown his hat beneath a loafer's bench and pushed it snug against the hotel's white clapboard wall where it remained, its crisp brim bending.

Longarm cupped a hand to his mouth, and yelled,

"Marshal Scobie? Federal lawman, here. It's peaceable out here now!"

Silence. The sun hammered the front of the hotel, reflecting off the broken windowpanes.

"I'm comin' in," Longarm said and started forward.

He stepped onto the broad, roofed boardwalk, pulled open the screen door, and tried the knob of the inside door. Locked. Letting the screen door slap shut, Longarm walked over to the window left of it and crouched to peer inside the hotel's saloon.

Dark in there, with several webs of powder smoke. Lots of bullet holes in tables and chairs and the mahogany bar and back bar to Longarm's left. The back bar mirror was shattered, as were most of the bottles and glasses on its shelves. In the dinginess, near an overturned, bullet-riddled table, an old, gray-haired man in baggy duck trousers and suspenders lay facedown on the floor, in a broad pool of brown blood.

A Henry rifle lay on the floor to his right, amidst countless empty shell casings.

Longarm used his rifle barrel to break out a sharp, triangular glass shard from the window's lower frame, then stepped through the window and inside the saloon. His boots crunched the broken glass on the floor. Holding his rifle straight out from his right hip, he looked around carefully.

Something moved on his left, and he swung his rifle toward the bar. A head ducked down.

"Come on outta there!" Longarm ordered.

"Don't shoot!" came the tremulous reply.

The head reappeared—just a cap of black hair and two brown eyes. Then the entire, black-mustached face rose from behind the bar, and the portly, round-faced man stood with his arms raised, his eyes dancing between Longarm's rifle and the copper badge pinned to the lawman's vest.

"Who're you?" Longarm said with a flint-eyed snarl.

"Florin. I own this place." The barman's gaze flicked across the bullet-riddled room toward the broad, carpeted staircase rising at the rear. "What's left of it . . ."

"That Scobie?"

The man nodded. "I'd appreciate it if you'd put that rifle down."

"You see the badge?"

"I could find a badge. If I wanted one badly enough."

"Where's Mrs. Pritchard?" Longarm said.

"Upstairs."

Poor woman, Longarm absently mused. Because of the wooden leg, she'd probably had trouble finding a husband. On top of *that* misery, all this . . .

"Anyone else here?"

As if in reply to Longarm's query, boots thumped in the ceiling, making their way across the second story over Longarm's head, toward the stairs. Longarm raised his rifle to his shoulder and aimed at the top of the stairs.

"Who's that?"

"That's Leroy," the barman said just as a young man with longish, curly blond hair appeared at the top of the stairs, starting down and holding a pistol in his right hand.

"Found Kirby's old six-shooter," the kid said, hurrying down the stairs, one hand on the rail. "It was right where you said it was . . ." The voice stopped suddenly, and he let his voice trail off. His eyes had found Longarm and turned sharp with fear.

"Drop the gun, Junior," Longarm ordered, aiming down the Winchester's barrel.

"Ah, shit!" the kid intoned, crumpling his young face with fear and frustration. "Who the fuck are you?"

"Custis P. Long," Longarm said. "Deputy U.S. marshal out of Denver. Go ahead and set that pistol down nice an' easy, and we can continue the conversation more friendly-like."

"You a lawman?" the kid said, pulling his vest away to reveal the five-pointed star pinned to his shirt. "So am I!"

"That's Leroy," said the barman, still holding his hands above his head.

"Leroy Panabaker," the kid said. "Deputy town marshal of Snow Mound, Colorado Territory."

"Just the same, Leroy, you'll wanna stow that pistol somewhere. You don't need it now. The three curly wolves out yonder are as dead as the gray-suited gent on the porch." The kid didn't appear much over fifteen years old. He was short and so thin that even his snakeskin suspenders were having a hard time holding his trousers up on his lean hips. The big Colt holstered on his right hip looked far too big for him to carry around without falling over, much less for him to handle safely.

Deputy Panabaker's close-set eyes flashed in surprise as he wedged the Schofield behind his cartridge
belt, all the leather loops of which, Longarm noted,
were empty. *"You got 'em?"*

Longarm lowered the rifle. "That's right. But not before they got your boss, looks like."

The kid came slowly down the stairs, his gaze growing dark as his eyes found the sheriff lying dead on the
floor. "Poor old Marshal Scobie. He took a ricochet
just before I went upstairs looking for another gun and
more ammo." The kid deputy shook his head sadly.
"He's the one that give me this job, nigh on two years
ago, now. He saw I had a callin' and he give me a
chance."

"Two years ago?" Longarm said. "Good Lord—you
must've been twelve."

"Fourteen. No one else in town wanted the job, and
I may not look like much, Marshal Long, but I can
shoot the white out of a hawk's eye at four hundred
yards." He glanced at the barman, who'd finally lowered his hands and was walking out from behind his
bar, looking around with a stricken expression on his
soft, pale, black-mustached face. "Can't I, Al?"

"Look at my place," said Al.

"Where's Miss Pritchard?" Longarm asked the kid
as he shouldered his rifle and headed for the stairs.

"Room seven up yonder," Leroy said. "She's awful
scared, but she'll be glad to know we done took care o'
them gunnies."

Longarm gave a wry snort and climbed the stairs. On the second floor he stopped in front of the door with a brass number seven adorning its top panel. Hearing quick footsteps on the carpeted stairs at the end of the hall, Longarm rapped on the door.

"Uh . . . Marshal Long?"

Longarm glanced back the way he'd come, saw the kid taking long strides toward him, an anxious look on his face. On the other side of the door facing Longarm, a pistol cracked. A slug hammered through the door's upper panel.

Longarm felt the air curl just left of his face as the slug continued on across the hall and into the red-papered wall on the opposite side. As the gun cracked again, chewing more slivers from the door, Longarm threw himself to the right and dropped to a crouch, scowling.

"What the *hell*!"

As though in reply, a female voice screeched on the other side of the door, "Go away, you savages! I have a gun, and I know how to use it!"

"I forgot to tell you," Deputy Panabaker said, crouching and holding one hand up, as though to shield himself from a bullet. "She's got a gun, and she knows how to use it!"

"Thanks for that valuable bit of information, Leroy!"

Young Panabaker rammed his left shoulder against the wall and hotfooted it up to the edge of the woman's door. He angled his left hand down low and rapped once on the door before jerking his hand back behind the wall. "Miss Pritchard—all's well! We done greased all three o' them owlhoots outside, and the coast is clear. You can come out now."

"Who's out there with you?" came the crisp female voice from inside.

"Deputy United States Marshal Custis Long out of Denver, ma'am. I have a badge, if you want to see it."

"What about the others?"

"The other who?"

"The other trail wolves," cried the woman from behind the door. "You don't think there are just three, do you? Oh, Lord—I'm *doomed*!"

Longarm glanced at Panabaker cheeked up against the wall on the other side of the door and said, "Open the door, Miss Pritchard."

"It's all right, Miss Pritchard," Leroy gently assured the terrified woman. "Like I said, we done sent them three outside to hell with coal shovels." He swallowed. "If you'll pardon my French . . ."

Longarm heard the squawk of a floorboard on the other side of the door. Likely, the poor one-legged, old thing was trying to compose herself as she headed for the door. Probably still trying to choke back a heart stroke. The lock scraped. The knob turned. The bolt clicked. And the door opened, hinges squeaking like red-winged blackbirds.

"All right," came the woman's voice. "But you'd better be who you say you are."

Longarm looked into the room and blinked his eyes as if to clear them.

"Like I warned," said the incredibly gorgeous, young, full-bosomed blonde in a red-and-white, low-cut gingham dress standing about six feet back from the door, "I have this here gun. My boss gave it to me back in Pinecone, in case of just such a catastrophic situation as the one I find myself now facing." She raised the gun in both her pale, slender hands. "And if you try anything at all untoward, I'll drill you! I swear I will!"

Chapter 7

Longarm looked over the girl's right shoulder, widened his eyes, and winced as though spying a threat in one of the room's two windows. The girl fell for it. She'd no sooner turned her head to follow his gaze than he lunged forward and easily jerked the gun from her hand.

She gave an indignant cry and, turning too quickly forward, lost her balance and dropped onto the edge of the bed. Silky locks of honey-blond hair tumbled enticingly across her face that appeared deftly chiseled by a master sculptor. "Oh, you bastard!"

Holding her pistol in his hand, Longarm stared down at the girl, incredulous. "You're . . . Josephine Pritchard?"

She threw hair back and glared up at him through lime-green eyes in which copper sparks flashed. "Who else would I be? And give me back that gun, damn you.

Mr. Cable from the Stockmen's Bank in Pinecone gave it to me to defend myself with!"

Longarm let his puzzled albeit appreciative gaze drift down the girl's fine, cream neck. He allowed it to linger for a second or two on the well-filled bodice of her low-cut dress, noting a very light splash of freckles across her cleavage that owned the color of a nearly ripe peach. A primitive, involuntary warmth touched the lawman's loins. He continued sliding his eyes down the girl's flat belly to her legs, the fine outlines of which he could see beneath her long, gingham skirt. Both were long, slender, and supple.

Obviously, neither was wooden.

Longarm chuckled. Did Billy really know what the girl looked like, or had he been merely trying to prepare his senior deputy for the worst possibility? Likely, the former.

Somehow, he'd gotten a description of the girl and, knowing Longarm's weakness for the fairer sex, had decided to jerk the randy lawman's chain. In Billy's conniving way, the ruse had probably also been meant to warn Longarm to keep his hands, as well as other more insistent body parts, off and out of the girl.

"Oh, God," the girl cried, wrinkling her thin, blond brows as she stared up at the big lawman towering over her, raking his eyes across every inch of her. "You're not only uncouth but crazy, to boot!"

"Easy, miss," Longarm said, poking her pistol into the waistband of his pants and regaining his composure. "I'm no more dangerous than your average coyote dog—

as long as you don't prod me with sticks or guns, I keep my hackles down." He turned to Deputy Leroy Panabaker standing just inside the door, blushing as he stared in unconscious admiration at the beautiful, disheveled, young creature on the bed near Longarm. "How many more o' them trail wolves, as Miss Pritchard calls 'em, is lurkin' around out there, Leroy?"

The boy turned slowly toward Longarm, lower jaw hanging. "What's that?"

"How many more o' them Younger gang is on the lurk, Deputy?" Longarm repeated, raising his voice to break the young badge toter out of his stupor.

"Twenty, at least," the girl answered.

Deputy Panabaker patted down the rooster tail at the crown of his skull and frowned. "There can't be that many. When I was up at Miss Barbara's place, I only counted fifteen or so."

"Where's Miss Barbara's place?" Longarm asked.

"About five miles up Old Burn Canyon, south of here. That's where the gang is holed up. They been sending a few men at a time to town to cause trouble— mess up the train tracks, shoot up saloons, and take potshots at the hotel where Miss Pritchard's been holed up since the two Pinkertons brought her to town to testify against old Babe Younger. They killed Detective Ramsay just last week—leastways, it was likely the gang that ambushed him from a dark alley when he was bringin' Miss Pritchard a supper tray."

"Those Younger savages were tryin' to scare and bedevil me, I reckon," the girl said, crossing her pretty legs and giving one foot a shake as she folded her arms on her chest. "And the rest of the town, too—for holding the trial for that awful varmint in the first place! But now, just this morning, they killed Mr. Andrews, the second Pinkerton, and stormed over here promising to hang me from the same gallows on which the town hanged Babe Younger!"

She sobbed and, scrunching up her face in horror, threw her head back, and howled. "After they took me back to that brothel in the canyon and let each of the gang take his turn with me!" She shook her head as tears streamed down her peaches-and-cream cheeks. "Oh, God—*I am truly doomed to a fate worse than death!*"

"Ah, you ain't doomed, Miss Pritchard."

Longarm shifted his feet uncomfortably, staring at the poor, bereaved creature sobbing before him. Finally, awkwardly, he sagged down on the edge of the bed. He wasn't sure he should put his arm around her. The gesture might only repel her further. But she obviously needed comforting. He steeled himself for the worst, laid his rifle down on the bed beside him, and snaked his left arm around her slender shoulders.

He felt like a varmint as low and seedy as the Younger gang for what the girl's warm, yielding flesh did to his nether regions as well as his imagination. But he gave her a little squeeze, just the same, and tried to keep his thoughts on business.

To his surprise, rather than jerk away from him, screaming, she suddenly turned to face him, throwing her arms around his thick neck and burying her face in his chest. Her firm breasts pushed against his belly, stirring the strong-willed old snake lurking in his trousers.

"Please don't let them have me, sir," she pleaded, shoulders quivering. "I'm all alone up here—just a poor girl from Pinecone working in Mr. Cable's fine bank to help support my family, and I thought I was doing right by testifying against those privy rats. They killed Mr. Lewis, after all!"

"Mr. Lewis?"

"The vice president and chief loan officer," she said. "Shot him right before my eyes. Even sprayed my blouse with *blood*!" She sobbed hysterically, finally catching her breath a little. "And now . . . and now they want to do the same to me, but even *worse*!" A few more sobs as she soaked the front of Longarm's shirt and vest with salty tears. "And no one . . . *no one can save me*!"

"Ah, now, that ain't true, neither, miss," Longarm said, gently rocking the girl and patting her fragile back. "That's what they sent me here to do—to see that you make it back down the mountains to your home in Pinecone—and that's exactly what I'm gonna do."

He glanced over at Deputy Panabaker staring at him, the kid's brows furled jealously.

"Deputy, go pick me an' Miss Pritchard out two of the finest horses in town. Speedsters with bottom and hearts like Baldwin locomotives."

The young deputy's expression turned incredulous. "Ain't you gonna wait on the train?"

"They clear the tracks yet?"

"Should be clear by tomorrow. We just got word this mornin'."

Longarm shook his head. "Me and Miss Pritchard are lighting out this afternoon. We're gonna find a back way to Pinecone, and hightail it. If that gang is only five miles away—I don't care how much fun they're having, they'll be ridin' in to find out what happened to those three in the street real soon. Besides, as slow as the trains are in this neck of the mountains, they'd run us down before their horses broke out in sweats."

Miss Pritchard lifted her head from Longarm's chest. "What are you proposing?"

"We're gonna make a run for it."

"Me?" She pulled her body away from his and crossed her arms on her breasts as though to cover them. "How do I know I can trust you?"

"I don't reckon it much matters. My assignment is to see you safely home, and that's what I intend to do. What're you just standin' there for, Leroy? Fetch those hosses—best ones in town. I don't care who owns 'em—this is federal business and Uncle Sam will pay for 'em. And we're gonna need a bag of grub—whatever you can find. Coffee and jerky oughta do it."

The boy stood in front of the door, looking indignant.

Longarm said, "Oh, and fetch me a few boxes of .44 shells, too, will you?" He scowled. "Leroy—have you gone deaf on me, son?"

The scowl lines deepened in the kid's face. "I . . . well . . . I ain't your errand boy, Marshal Long. Me— well, hell, I'm a deputy town marshal! And now I reckon, since Marshal Scobie done rode over the Divide, I'm head lawman of the entire town of Snow Mound." He puffed up his chest a little and thrust out his chin. "Yes, sir! I ain't your errand boy."

Longarm stood, trying to keep from blowing his stack. "I do apologize, ki . . . I mean, Marshal Panabaker. Seein' as how we're short on time and we want to get the young lady to safety as soon as possible, do you think you could maybe help me out? I don't know the layout of the town, you see, and . . ."

"Well, all right." The kid stood ramrod straight and looked at Miss Pritchard as he said, "I reckon it beats you wastin' a bunch of time, stumblin' around lookin' for horses and grub an' such. I'll be happy to help you out, Marshal Long. But you federal boys have to understand who's in charge around here. And right now that's me, you see?"

"I see that, Marshal. And I am truly obliged you're helpin' me out of this pinch. When I get back to Denver, I'll make sure Chief Marshal Billy Vail writes you up a commendation."

"No kiddin'?"

"I don't kid in situations such as this, Juni . . . I mean, Marshal Panabaker."

"Do you think he could get the governor to sign it? My ma'd be awful thrilled to—"

"You bet your boots, the governor'll sign it. I'm sure he'd be happy to." Longarm drew a deep, calming breath. "As long as me and Miss Pritchard here can get out of town *soon* . . . and in one *piece* . . . !"

"Oh, of course, o' course!" The kid jerked around, hitching his pistol belt higher on his hips. "I'll meet you out on the street with fresh horses, grub, and ammo in a half hour!"

Longarm turned to the girl, who stared up at him accusingly. "Marshal Scobie said he'd sent for U.S. marshals. Why is there only one of you?"

"'Cause that's all it's gonna take." Longarm winked at the girl and sauntered over to the door, trying to look more confident than he actually felt. "Now, you'd best pack and get ready to go. We're pullin' out in a half hour."

He went out and closed the door behind him.

"I'm doomed," he heard the girl say thinly behind him. "This is the surefire end of little Miss Josephine Pritchard."

"Thanks for the vote of confidence," the lawman muttered as he headed for the stairs.

He headed on outside and took a close look around, making sure no more of Younger's curly wolves were in the immediate vicinity. Spying no one but a few shopkeepers willing now to brave the outdoors in the wake of the lead storm, and the collie sitting proprietarily near the charred body of the man who'd intended to set fire to the hotel, Longarm tramped out behind the saloon and returned to the hotel with the big roan in tow.

In the main saloon hall, while the barman dragged the dead marshal outside and laid him beside the dead Pinkerton, Longarm found one of the few lone, unbroken bottles behind the bar and poured himself a drink. He sat at a table with a good view of the street, propped his feet on a chair, and sipped the whiskey while he reloaded his weapons, taking the time to dismantle his Colt and clean it with an oily cloth from his saddlebags.

Both weapons were going to come in handy if there were a dozen or so more gang members after Miss Pritchard, and if they were all holed up in a canyon only five miles from Snow Mound. If luck was smiling on Longarm, they were all down with the bottle flu or otherwise indisposed, and it would take them a while to come looking for their dead cohorts.

As he slipped the cleaned and oiled cylinder back into his Colt with a satisfying click, and spun it, he wondered when the three dead men had been expected to report back with Miss Pritchard thrown over one of their saddles as a trophy of sorts.

Longarm tipped back a bracing sip of the whiskey and turned his thoughts to the girl. He chuffed. Damn Billy. Longarm knew the lie about the girl's age and her wooden leg was his boss's way of indirectly—since directness had never worked in the past—warning his badge-toting underling to keep his mitts to himself, in spite of the girl's incredible, green-eyed, pert-breasted beauty.

Screwing around on the job was a might unprofessional. That wouldn't likely be a problem up here, however. The girl might be an enticing little morsel, but both she and Longarm had more important things to think about than fleshly satisfaction.

Like, for instance, keeping their flesh free of lead.

Damn, where was that kid and the horses . . . ?

Longarm dropped his feet to the floor, stood, and walked over to the batwings. He looked around and saw the kid moving toward him from the east. Deputy Marshal Panabaker was riding a big, white-socked black gelding while leading a coyote dun and a claybank. Leroy's black was fully rigged with a bedroll, saddlebags, and the scarred stock of an old Spencer rifle jutting from a leather scabbard tied to the saddle beneath the kid's right leg.

Longarm heard footsteps behind him and turned to see Josephine Pritchard descending the stairs, a carpetbag in each hand. She wore gloves and a little straw hat with fake berries and leaves, black boots, and a short-waisted rabbit coat.

"Thanks for the horses, Marshal," Longarm said, removing his saddlebags from the roan's back and slinging them over the back of the claybank.

"Yeah, these oughta do us."

Longarm had his back to the kid. To his left, on the other side of the street, the barman and the whores stood outside the saloon, watching him and the kid with mute interest. Up and down the street he saw three other people—shopkeepers in shirtsleeves and aprons—standing like sullen sentinels on their stoops or boardwalks, watching, likely just wanting Longarm and the girl to get on out of Snow Mound and leave them to the peace and quiet of this high-mountain town.

He wished only to oblige them.

He glanced at the kid sitting the black. "No 'us' in it, Marshal. Just me and the girl." He glanced over at her standing on the boardwalk, casting wary glances up and down the street.

"You're gonna need help, Marshal Long," the kid said, trying to pitch his youthful-raspy voice with authority. "I best ride along and make sure you make it safe. Like I said, I can shoot the white out of a hawk's eye—"

"With Marshal Scobie dead, you're needed here," Longarm said, taking the carpetbags from the girl and hanging both by their braided leather lanyards over the coyote dun's saddle horn. "But I do appreciate the offer."

The kid scowled as Longarm returned to the boardwalk, grabbed the girl's arm, and led her over to the coyote dun. When the young badge toter opened his mouth to press the matter, Longarm bit back a sharp retort and the urge to drag the kid out of his saddle and paddle the hell out of him, and said with a deferential smile, "I know the citizens of Snow Mound will be right happy to have you here when the Younger gang comes lookin' for the girl. I reckon they'll be too hard after us to cause much trouble, but I know my heart will feel lighter, having you here to sort of smooth things over."

"Yeah, I . . . I reckon," the kid said noncommittally, glancing around at the barman and the whores and the shopkeepers all staring toward him, Longarm, and the girl. "I reckon someone needs to stay here an' take charge . . . with the marshal dead."

Longarm leaned down, picked the girl up in his arms, and set her in the saddle. The hem of her dress drew taut.

"We're gonna have to rig you a ridin' dress," Longarm said, producing a folding barlow knife from his pants pocket. "Don't be alarmed."

He opened the blade, pulled the girl's dress out away from her fine, long, left leg, and quickly slit it with the knife. No, that leg wasn't wooden, he saw, a cold stone of desire dropping in his belly. Not long by a shot!

He didn't look at Marshal Panabaker, but he thought he heard the kid groan.

The girl gasped and quickly reached down to pull the cut material over her naked thigh. "You enjoyed that!" she hissed.

Longarm turned away from the girl to cover his guilty smile. He swung up into the claybank's saddle. "Now, Juni . . . I mean, Marshal Panabaker—if you'll just point out the best route down the mountains to Pinecone, me and Miss Pritchard will be on our way."

The kid did, albeit reluctantly and while staring at the girl, whose main concern was the Younger gang.

Longarm and the girl rode at spanking trots out of town. Just beyond the little settlement, and as they headed into a narrow canyon mouth, Longarm glanced behind to see the young marshal of Pinecone still sitting the black, staring after him and, likely, the most beautiful creature he'd ever laid eyes on.

Chapter 8

After an hour's hard ride up a meandering trail through a narrow canyon and then along the shoulder of a steep mountain, Longarm crested a saddle, and reined in the claybank. He stepped out of the saddle as the girl galloped up behind him.

Her hat had blown off, and her hair was a silky tumbleweed after the long, hard pull up the canyon. She was rosy-cheeked, and her eyes were glazed from fear and the chill breeze, but he'd been happy to see she could ride. Having to give her a crash course on horsemanship would have wasted precious time.

"Wait here," the lawman said, dropping the claybank's reins. "I'm gonna check our backtrail."

He strode up a rocky rise and dropped to a knee. Instantly, his belly drew up in a knot. On the other side of a secondary ridge, black smoke rose into the clear, blue vault of the Colorado sky. As he watched, he saw that there were actually three separate smoke plumes rising to form one billowy, black cloud over the canyon in which Snow Mound sat.

"Shit." Longarm raked a frustrated hand down his jaw. "Why in the hell'd you have to do that?"

"Do what?"

He glanced over his shoulder. Holding her skirts above her black boots, the girl was striding up the knoll behind him. "I told you to stay there."

"Why did they have to what, Deputy Long?" she insisted, moving up to stand beside him.

Longarm rose and grabbed her arm. "Don't stand up there like that. You're liable to get spotted."

She pulled her arm loose and hardened her jaws angrily. "Why did they do *what*?" She stared out over the rolling, pine-carpeted ridges. He saw her back tighten. Her shoulders rose and fell as she breathed. The wind blew her hair back. Suddenly, her knees buckled and hit the ground.

"Oh, no!" she cried.

Longarm lunged for her, wrapped an arm around her, and pulled her back to her feet. "It's not your fault."

She was shivering as he led her back down the knoll toward the horses. "Whose is it, then?" she said weakly, her voice brittle with self-recrimination.

"It's the fault of those who torched the town," he said, rage burning through him. "They'll pay. Maybe not now, but they will soon. You get back on your horse. They're likely working up behind us now, and we need to hightail it."

She was sobbing, shoulders jerking, as she stood facing her horse, one hand on the stirrup fender, the other on the cantle. "I never should have testified!"

"You did testify." Longarm lifted her into the saddle and gave her the dun's reins. "And it was the right thing to do. Now, unless you wanna give in to those killers, let 'em kill you and me, too, you have to follow me and keep up. You understand, Miss Pritchard?"

She was squeezing her eyes shut, and tears welled out from behind them to stream down her cheeks, glistening in the cool, brassy sunshine. The wind dried them before they reached her straight, delicate jaws.

Longarm wrapped a hand on both of hers that rested, one atop the other, on her saddle horn.

"You understand, Miss Pritchard? Otherwise, those killers are gonna win."

She sucked a ragged breath, opened her eyes, and looked at him. Slowly, she nodded, then ran the back of her hand across her cheeks. "Okay." She drew another bracing draught of the cool, dry air. "I'll follow. I'll keep up to you, Marshal Long."

Longarm reined the claybank around and ground his heels into the beasts's flanks, moving off at a trot along the wagon trace that, according to the government survey maps he'd studied on the train, led to several small mining encampments dotting the mountains. He recognized several surrounding peaks, and used them to keep his bearings as the trail wound down another mountain shoulder, then flattened out in a fur-choked canyon.

They couldn't keep to the trail for long. Their sign was too obvious, too easily followed.

When he came to a narrow creek that crossed the trail and over which someone had built a simple, halved-log bridge, he reined the dun to another stop. To his left, the stream tumbled down a series of terraces, its source probably far up the mountain. To his right, the streambed shallowed and broadened as it carved a path through a crease between two slopes.

There was no trail there, other than game trails. Which made it a good route for two people on the run from a gang that badly outnumbered them.

"Come on," he told the girl, and put the claybank into the stream.

"Why are we riding in the creek?" she asked behind him, as the horses splashed through the fetlock-deep water, in which the slender, dark shapes of trout darted away like shadows.

"Cover our sign." He stopped the horse, dismounted, and broke a branch off a young pine, low enough down that the fresh wound in the trunk wouldn't be obvious. "Keep going," he told Miss Pritchard, watching him dubiously. "I'll be along in a minute."

As the girl batted her heels against the dun's flanks and went splashing down the rippling streambed, Long-arm walked back up the stream. Without leaving the streambed, the cold water running over his boots and soaking his legs halfway up to his knees, he used the branch to obliterate their tracks, where they curved off the wagon trail and into the creek. Not a foolproof maneuver, but one that might buy them some extra time for losing the gang in the off-trail slopes and wooded canyons.

He tossed the branch into a chokecherry snag and removed his hat to look at the sky. The sun was a buttery-gold ball balanced atop the peak of a high, western ridge, sending javelins of shimmering rays eastward. The sun would be down soon—a good bit of luck. The diminishing light would be in Longarm's favor, as his and the girl's trail would be harder to follow. But it also meant the mountain cold was on its way, and he'd have to find a place to camp and build a fire. Miss Pritchard wasn't dressed for a cold spring mountain night.

Longarm tramped through the frigid water tumbling down the mountain. Just as he reached for the dun's reins, which he'd wrapped around his saddle horn, he froze. He'd heard something.

Turning to look over his right shoulder, toward the trail dropping down the timbered slope behind him, he heard it again—the clatter of galloping hooves. Men's voices rose, muted by the stream. Longarm's heart thudded. He stepped back from the horse, peering up the slope through the trees.

He couldn't see the riders, but their thudding hooves grew louder.

"Shit!"

He swung up into the leather and put the dun into a gallop upstream. The girl was ahead of him, walking downstream. She glanced over her shoulder as he approached, and her eyes quickly regained their old horror.

"What is it?"

"Follow me."

He splashed past the girl on the coyote dun, following the stream as it turned slightly toward the right, dropping gradually but steadily. Up the left slope, a knob of granite jutted from the northern slope. Longarm put the claybank up the left bank and, glancing back to make sure the girl was still behind him, continued on up the slope through spindly birches and aspens cloaked in small, lime-green, spring leaves.

When he and the girl were behind the escarpment, Longarm dropped out of the saddle and shucked his Winchester from the scabbard. "Stay back," he said as he scrambled along the pitted rock wall. "And keep down."

"They're coming, aren't they?" she said tonelessly behind him.

He dropped to a knee beside the wall and glanced back at her. She sat the dun, half turned toward him. Her face was as white as a sheet. He tried to give her a reassuring look, quirking the corners of his mouth slightly, and pressed two fingers to his lips.

Gripping the Winchester tightly in his hands, and hearing the loudening thuds of the oncoming riders, he edged a look around the knob, staring back along the creek toward where the trail came down the slope and crossed the bridge. He didn't have to wait long before the first horsebackers came into view, riding hard down the slope, partly curtained by the forest of columnar lodgepole pines and firs.

The horses were blowing and snorting, legs scissoring. Their withers were lathered. The first two men were big and unshaven, and guns bristled about their buckskin or calico-clad frames. The man nearest Longarm was beefy, and he wore a blond beard and a high-crowned Stetson with a Texas crease. Cartridge bandoliers crisscrossed his chest. The brass shells flashed in the sunlight angling down the steep slope on the other side of the trail.

The man galloping beside him wore a shabby bowler hat and buckskins. Thick, dark muttonchops ran down the sides of his face. He carried a double-barreled shotgun across his saddlebows as he rode, leaning forward in his saddle and just now spitting to one side as he and the other man raced across the bridge.

They continued on across the creek and then disappeared behind the knob as they headed north along the canyon, the other riders following, occasionally yelling, their horses' racing hooves kicking up a rataplan cacophony in the wooded hollow, the thudding on the bridge sounding like sporadic drum rolls.

Longarm raked his gaze across the other men in the pack. He counted thirteen. All looked as savage and determined as the first two riders.

Longarm raked his thumb eagerly across the Winchester's hammer. He'd have loved nothing more than to raise the long gun and commence blowing the killers and town burners out of their saddles. But doing so would be suicide.

Eventually, the men would die. He'd have Billy assign a few more lawmen, building up a good-sized posse, and with them upping his odds, Longarm would hunt them all and kill them or send them to the gallows where they'd stretch hemp in the same fashion as their kill-crazy leader.

He was glad when they'd drifted on past the creek and his and the girl's position behind the granite scarp. The temptation to open fire was gone. Now, he needed to get the girl into a safe camping site and build a fire. Already, he could feel the cold descending as the light quickly waned.

He turned to her. She sat her horse as before, looking gaunt and pale. She was also shivering—he could see her shoulders jerking slightly under her short, rabbit-fur coat.

"Let's go," he said, grabbing the claybank's reins and stepping into the saddle. "We'll keep heading up this canyon, find a place to hole up for the night."

"Soon . . . they'll see we're no longer ahead of them," she said, her voice brittle, toneless.

"Yeah, they will." Longarm rested his rifle across his saddlebows. "But by that time it'll be dark as a glove down here, and they'll have no way of tracking us. Won't be a moon for several nights yet." He offered another reassuring smile, trying hard to make it look authentic. "Come on, Miss Pritchard. We're gonna be all right."

"There's so many of them," she said in that same, depressed tone, staring with glazed eyes over Longarm's shoulder. "You're only one man . . ."

"Come on, Miss Pritchard," he said, reining his horse back into the canyon. "Like I said, we're gonna be just fine."

As he swung the gelding up canyon, he hated the uncertainty he heard in his voice.

Chapter 9

The fire's glow flickered across the fine curve of the
girl's naked leg. Longarm let his eyes roam down the
smooth flesh, colored copper by the wavering light of
the small fire he'd built in the hollow, a good five miles
or so from where they'd entered the creek.

Longarm sipped the coffee he'd laced with rye and
chuckled to himself. Wooden, eh, Billy? He swallowed
the spicy, bracing brew, enjoying the heat of it flooding
his stomach and sending the warmth all through his
limbs, staving off the night's deep, frosty chill.

He leaned forward, admiring the leg once more,
then drew the blanket down over it, keeping her warm.
She'd been asleep for a couple of hours now. She
hadn't accepted any of the jerky or bread or coffee that
Longarm had offered, after they'd made camp here in
this narrow, stone- and brush-choked canyon.

She hadn't spoken, either. Not a good sign, he thought. She was scared. But more than scared, she was horrified by what had happened as a result of her testifying against Babe Younger. He'd wanted to reassure her that she'd done the right thing, and that the killing of the Pinkertons and Marshal Scobie as well as the burning of the town of Snow Mound—had others died, then, too?—had not been her fault.

It had been the fault of those who had done the actual burning and killing.

But he knew that in her withdrawn sadness and terror, his words wouldn't have reached her. So he'd said nothing, only made a good soft bed for her of pine boughs and blankets, positioning her saddle for a pillow, and watched her roll up in the bed and drift into the sanctuary of sleep.

Up the narrow canyon a ways, one of the horses snorted. Longarm looked to see them both standing just beyond the edge of the firelight, one swishing its tail in relative contentment while the other stood statue still, brown tail hanging. He could see the soft clouds of their breath puffing above their heads.

It was a still, quiet night. Cold as the moon. The stars were so bright, seemed so close, that he should be able to reach up and grab them. The air smelled of cold stone and pine resin as well as the smoke from his fire. His coffeepot gurgled and chugged on a flat rock to one side. It was a small fire, one that couldn't be seen outside of ten or fifteen yards. The smoke was shredded about ten feet above, where a stone ledge angled out away from the ridge behind him.

He was relatively certain they wouldn't be discovered here. Not with the night as black as it was. Tomorrow would be another story. They'd have to move out early, at the first blush of dawn. He intended to hide out here in these mountains until he was sure the gang had given up on him, and then take the girl back to Denver.

He'd convince Billy she needed protective custody until Longarm and a well-armed, experienced posse could run them all to ground. She'd never be safe until every last one of the Babe Younger gang was kicked out with a cold shovel.

There was no point in taking her home, because she wouldn't be safe there. Denver was the only place. He hadn't told her that, and he wouldn't until he thought she could handle the information. Now, she likely only wanted the perceived safety of her home in Pinecone, and telling her she couldn't go back to her family, or whoever she had there, would probably only drive her over the edge.

Longarm sipped his coffee and stared at the girl. She lay curled on her side, facing away from him and the fire, her blankets pulled up around her neck. All he could see was her golden-blond hair, a little of her peach-colored cheek across which the fire's shadows played. He felt sorry for the girl. She'd been brave to testify against Babe Younger. Few men would have done such a thing. But she'd done her duty as a citizen, and she'd paid the price for it.

Unfortunately, it looked like she wasn't done paying for it.

Longarm owed it to her to keep her safe until he could return her safely home.

As though she'd just realized the long trek ahead, she sighed, blowing strands of hair out away from her cheek. She shifted a little in the blanket, which slid off her shoulder. Longarm stood, moved around the fire, and pulled the blanket up snug against her neck. She gave another sigh, and then her slow, heavy breaths resumed.

Longarm finished off his coffee and whiskey, set another small log on the fire, then grabbed his Winchester from where it leaned against the high, stone ridge. Time to have a look around. Rifle in hand, he walked quietly away from the fire so not to wake the girl and followed the game trail they'd followed in here, to the canyon mouth.

He dropped to a knee amongst the rocks that disguised the opening. The main canyon stretched perpendicular to the one he and the girl were camped in; it was as black as the bottom of a deep well. No sounds except for the distant hooting of an owl.

There was a distant flicker of light that Longarm first thought was the reflection of starlight off the stream that cut through the far side of the broader, main canyon. As he stared at it, however, he saw that it was not reflected starlight at all.

It was the orange glow of a campfire amongst the

trees lining the stream about a hundred yards down canyon, to Longarm's right.

Longarm drew a deep breath, held it, then let it out slow. There was a good chance whoever was camped out there was not after him and the girl. Woodcutters or hunters or the like.

On the other hand, there was a good chance the gang had split up to comb the mountains, and the campfire belonged to one such faction. If the entire gang was camped out there, there would be more fires.

Well, there was only one way to find out. And possibly cull the pack some, maybe even gather a couple of spare horses to ease the strain on the dun and claybank young Panabaker had picked out for Longarm and the girl . . .

Longarm poked his hat brim off his forehead and stared at the fire. It probably wasn't a risk he should take. If he should buy the farm, the girl would be on her own and relatively defenseless. On the other hand, he couldn't resist the urge to check out the camp yonder. Even on foot—a horse would make too much noise—it wouldn't take him long. If he saw he was too badly outnumbered, he'd hotfoot it back to the fire.

He returned to the camp where the girl slept beneath the ledge and added a couple more logs to the fire. Then he headed back down the game path and into the main canyon, striding quickly but as quietly as possible, wishing he had a good pair of Indian moccasins to make the trek even quieter. He moved at an angle to the stream, figuring the sound of the water pouring over rocks and occasional beaver dams would drown any noise he'd make.

He headed upstream, crouching, trying to keep as many trees as possible between himself and the distant glow. Slowly, the fire grew in size before him, blotted out occasionally by thickets and trees as he moved, following the crooked bed of the stream.

He stepped between two birches. A pistol-like crack sounded behind him. He crouched and spun, clicking the Winchester's hammer back, heart racing. Then he saw the gray-brown blur of the deer dashing off through the brush on the other side of the creek, heard the thud of its hooves as it bounded away up a southern feeder canyon, snapping twigs as it fled.

He spun forward again and dropped to a knee.

His heart started to slow, but apprehension tore like sharp talons at the back of his neck. Had the men in the camp heard the deer?

He held his position, his ears almost aching with the strain of listening for the slightest sound. When all he heard was the subtle chuckling of the stream, and decided that the deer he'd flushed had not been heard or considered a concern, he rose and continued striding forward.

The fire grew until he could see sparks wheeling and sputtering above the dancing flames. He got down and crawled, moving one hand, one knee at a time, holding his rifle just above the ground and stopping every few steps to look carefully around. From ahead, three separates sets of snores rose. When he was just beyond the edge of the firelight, he rose to his knees behind a large cottonwood, and looked around its left side.

He'd been right. Three men. There might be a picket or two, but he didn't think so, as there were only three sets of blanket rolls and tack.

Carefully, he perused the camp. The three men lay within a few feet of the fire they'd built and banked. He could see the bearded face of only one of the trio and recognized him from the wolf pack he'd seen earlier. The other two had their backs to him. Both lay on their sides, their shoulders rising and falling as their raucous snores lifted, clear in the silent night air. Rifles lay within quick grabbing distance, as did their boots.

Longarm drew his head back behind the tree.

Three was a manageable number given that they were all asleep. But there was no telling how far away the others in the pack were. Probably not within a mile or so, as this was a big, rugged country, and the splinter groups would need to put some distance between each other to give the separate canyons and watersheds a thorough scouring.

Still, he'd use his guns as a last . . .

One of the men coughed and grunted. Longarm heard the rustling of blankets, the squawk of a cartridge belt. He pressed his shoulder hard against the tree, trying to make himself as small as possible, so he wouldn't be seen from the camp.

The man coughed and grunted again, and Longarm heard the man's knees pop as he rose from his bedroll.

"Ah, fuck," the man groaned.

Longarm squeezed the rifle in his hands, held it tight straight up and down in front of him, gritting his teeth. While the other two men continued snoring, the man who'd risen muttered something Longarm couldn't hear. The lawman saw the man's shadow slide across the ground to his right, moving toward his covering tree.

Longarm ground his molars together and clamped his thumb over the Winchester's hammer as he heard the soft thuds of stocking feet moving toward him. The man's groans and muttered curses grew louder, and then Longarm smelled the rancid horse sweat of the man as he passed about six inches off Longarm's right shoulder. He stepped out into the night and stopped about six feet from the crouching lawman.

The man fumbled around in front of himself and then threw his head back and flexed his knees. He had thick, curly, dark-red hair though there was a bald spot at the top of his head about the size of a silver cartwheel. He wore a pistol on his right thigh; a big bowie knife was sheathed on his left.

A dribbling sound rose. A stream of piss shone between the killer's spread legs, angling onto the leaves and pine needles in front of his feet clad in torn socks. The pee steamed in the chill air.

Longarm knew what he was going to do without thinking about it. Lifting his rifle butt-forward, he stepped straight out away from the tree and rammed the butt plate as hard as he could against the back of the man's neck.

There was a cracking sound as the man's head snapped back on his shoulders. It hung crooked as he sighed and stumbled forward, continuing to pee. The man dropped to his knees, remained there, head hanging awkwardly for a full five seconds. As he started to sag forward, Longarm reached out and grabbed the back of his shirt collar, eased him slowly onto the ground.

He lay still on the ground damp from his own piss—instantly dead of a broken neck.

One of the other two men stirred behind him, rasping, "What the hell was that?"

Chapter 10

Longarm grabbed the bowie knife from the dead man's belt sheath, whipped around, and saw one of the other two men by the fire reaching for his rifle. The lawman bounded forward, past the tree, and flipped the blade by the end of its staghorn handle. Longarm hadn't thrown a knife in a month of Sundays, but it was an automatic maneuver, and the knife flashed end over end through the tops of the dancing flames.

There was a thumping crunch.

The man on the other side of the fire wheezed and dropped the rifle as he looked down at the knife handle sticking out of his chest. Longarm didn't wait to see the effects of his throw. The third killer, who lay to the far left side of the fire, had just lifted his head and was blinking his eyes. As he rose onto his arms, Longarm strode the last few feet. The man's eyes widened when he saw the big man lunging toward him. Before he could even begin to reach for his rifle leaning against his saddle, Longarm swung his Winchester like a club. It smashed against the side of the man's head with the sound of a branch breaking, crushing his skull.

The man whipped over onto his side and jerked as the life sputtered from his badly damaged brain.

Longarm slipped into the shadows just beyond the fire and dropped to a knee, looking around and listening for any possible pickets running back to see what all the commotion had been about. There were no sounds at all—not even the distant yips of a coyote or the screech of a hunting nighthawk. Even the horses that had been picketed beyond the fire stood still, all three looking toward Longarm, their eyes dully reflecting the fire's glow.

One stomped, then stretched its neck to nibble something from its hip. Longarm almost snorted at the horses' lack of concern for their dead owners.

He remained there on one knee, looking around, wanting to be certain he was alone out here before stepping back into the firelight where he'd be easy pickings with a rifle. Finally, he depressed the Winchester's hammer, returned to the fire, and kicked dirt on it, dousing it almost instantly, leaving only the wood glowing like volcanic rock to offer what little light he needed.

Quickly, wasting no movement—he wanted to get back to the girl as fast as possible—he saddled two of the dead killers' horses, setting the third one free of its picket line. He took one Winchester and a Colt .44 with handsomely carved peachwood grips and plundered a set of saddlebags for a spare box of .44 rifle rounds. With ten men on his trail, he could use all the extra firepower he could carry and still be relatively light on his feet.

Also amongst the men's gear he found spare, relatively clean clothing for the girl, a food bag containing a field-dressed jackrabbit and a burlap pouch of pinto beans. He stowed the duds, food, and ammo in one pair of saddlebags, draped the bags over one of the two horses he intended to steal—a mouse-brown dun with a four-pointed star on its face—and rode out away from the camp, leading the second horse by its reins. As he'd expected the third horse followed, unwilling to be left behind.

To keep the noise down, knowing how far sound carried in the mountains at night, he walked the horses back into the narrow canyon in which his fire still burned, albeit much lower than before, just a few small flames licking at the charred branches in the fire ring. As he passed the bivouac, he saw the girl's blond head lift from her saddle. She made a startled sound, and Longarm called to her, "All's well. Custis Long here with a few more horses to add to our cavvy."

He chuckled, not so much out of his finding humor in the situation but because his blood was up. Three men down.

Ten to go . . .

The next morning he got Miss Pritchard to eat a few bites of the rabbit he cooked on a spit he'd fashioned from two green willow branches. She accepted the cup of smoking coffee he gave her and watched him with mute interest for a time as they both ate.

Then she asked, canting her head up the narrow notch toward the five horses tied to his picket line, "So . . . where'd the three horses come from? Did you find a ranch out here?"

"Not exactly." Longarm bit off a hunk of the stringy but flavorful rabbit and chewed.

She swallowed a bite of the meat, blew ripples on her coffee, and took a small sip. "Not exactly . . ."

"Found three of the Younger gang camped out yonder, in the big canyon."

She stared at him over the steaming cup of coffee. It was false dawn, the hollow still filled with heavy shadows. It was as cold as it had been a few hours ago, but it would warm up fast as the sun climbed. Nearby, an owl hooted.

"And you . . . ?"

"Let's just say they've harassed their last murder witness." He thought of young Leroy Panabaker, and ground his jaws. "And burned their last town."

She stared at him, lips parted. Longarm grabbed the coat he'd taken from the killers' camp. In it, he'd wrapped some extra clothes. He tossed it across the fire to the girl. "There you go. Put those on. Keep you from catchin' a chill up on the high divide."

She looked at the bundle in front of her, then wrinkled a brow at Longarm. "High divide?"

"That's where we're headin'."

"I thought I was going home."

Longarm shook his head as he chewed. "They'll be expecting us to head down the watersheds to Pinecone. We're gonna do the opposite." He jerked a thumb at the gradually lightening sky. "We're heading up. Don't worry—it won't be for long. I figure they'll get bored with this vengeance quest of theirs. I'm sure Babe was a right good leader, but I figure they're mostly out here to terrorize you and anyone associated with you mainly for kicks and giggles. They burned the town, or part of the town, for the same reason. And meanness, of course. They're a nasty bunch. But they'll get bored out here after a couple of days, and head on back to Utah or wherever the hell they're from, find someone else to bother until I can throw a loop around 'em."

"What if they don't get bored, Deputy Long? What happens if they keep coming after us? I find your having taken down those three last night right admirable. Damned impressive, even. But do you actually think, if we can't outrun them, that you can kill them *all*?"

Longarm hiked a shoulder. "I reckon we'll have to see." He bit the last bit of rabbit meat off the leg bone and jerked his head toward the rocks rising on his left, near where the horses waited, swishing their tails. "Go on and put them duds on. Gonna get cold where we're goin', Miss Pritchard."

She gave a frustrated snort and looked at him pointedly. "My mother and father are going to be very worried about me. Especially after they hear what happened to the town of Snow Mound."

"Then they'll be all the more relieved when they finally see you walk through the front door again." He narrowed an eye at her. "That's all I'm tryin' to do, Miss Pritchard. Get you home safe and sound." He decided to play a card he'd hoped he could keep in his sleeve. "You wouldn't want us to lead that gang of town burners back to your hometown, would you? Maybe even to your folks' front door?"

She considered this, folding her upper lip over the brim of her coffee cup. Finally, with a fateful sigh, she set the cup down and picked up the bundle. She untied the sleeves of the buckskin mackinaw, making a face. "Smells like sweat," she sniped, then opened the coat and picked up the blue jeans. "Too long." She draped the jeans over her knee and picked up the plaid flannel shirt. "Way too big."

"The sleeves and cuffs you can roll up. I threw a rope in there—you can use that to keep your pants on. There's gloves there, too. Even some extra wool socks."

"Thought of everything didn't you?" she said coolly.

Longarm hiked a shoulder.

She pressed her lips together and shot him a snide look. "I suppose you'd like to put them on me, too?"

"You're a big girl. I figure you can dress yourself."

"I've seen the way you've looked at me."

"Now, I can't help that, can I? You're damn nice to look at."

"You're a big, lusty man—aren't you, Deputy Long?

I suppose there wouldn't be anything to stop you from having your way with me out here. There wouldn't be much I could do. Would there?"

"Nope." Longarm threw the last of his coffee back. "There'd probably be damn little you could do, except maybe kick and scream. But if I wanted to take you, I'd take you."

He ridged a brow and narrowed an eye at her. "Now, I don't mind you assuming the worst from me. I figure your experience with rough men has allowed you that. And make no mistake, I am a rough man. But I'm one of the ruffians on your side, and if you can't see that, there's nothing I can do about it."

He glanced at the sky. "The sun's gonna be up soon, and we need to get our tails on the trail. So, if you don't go back behind those rocks and put those clothes on real quick-like, I will put them on you myself and throw your pretty little ass into the saddle."

He stood and kicked dirt and rocks on the fire. "And, yes, I'd probably enjoy it!"

She gasped, picked up the clothes, clutching them and the coat to her breasts, and glaring at him over her shoulder, walked haughtily off into the rocks.

"Women!" Longarm raked out to himself as he began rolling up blankets and gathering gear. "Try to save their damn hides and they think you only want a piece of 'em . . ."

While he worked he glimpsed her head moving around behind the rocks as she dressed, tossing her hair across her naked shoulders. She met his glance once with a cool, defiant one of her own.

When he'd gathered up both of their saddles and saddle blankets, he walked past the rocks behind which she was dressing. She gasped, and out the corner of his eye he saw her clutch the coat to herself even though she was wearing the oversized shirt he'd brought her.

"Don't worry—I'm not after your precious body," he groused and continued over to the horses. He couldn't help adding as he threw the blanket over the coyote dun's back, "Not yet, anyways. Maybe I'll be requirin' payment a little later on."

"I wouldn't doubt it a bit," she said, throwing her hair out from the collar of the big mackinaw.

When he'd helped her into her saddle, neither meeting the other's gaze, he stepped into his own saddle and led the string down the narrow gorge and into the broader canyon beyond. He checked both ways carefully, to make sure no riders were about, then reined the claybank eastward along the valley, in the opposite direction from the camp in which the dead men lay, likely just now being pecked by crows and mountain jays.

As the sun rose, Longarm led the way along the valley until it intersected with another, then followed the other on a generally northward course, heading for a snow-mantled pass looming far above and ahead, at the top of a ridge cloaked in deep runnels, boulders, and clumps of pines and aspens that showed a lighter green than the conifers.

That was Grizzly Ridge—a famous landmark in this neck of the Colorado Rockies. A little mining town lay far down the other side—at least, there had been a town there when he'd passed north of the ridge a couple years ago—so there was a likely a way up and over the pass from here, or a canyon that led through it, though a quick perusal of his government survey maps showed none.

That was all right. If it was easy for him, it would be easy for the Babe Younger bunch. After a slow, careful look around while he and the girl paused to make coffee and rest the horses, he decided there was no better, wilder area in which to lose his pursuers.

Likely, they'd find the dead men soon, if they hadn't already. They'd be on his and the girl's trail within a couple of hours.

The sun was full up when Longarm discovered a notch in the side of Grizzly Ridge. It appeared little more than a vertical line sheathed in aspens, birches, and large boulders. But as he and the girl approached the bottom of the ridge two hours later, he saw that the crease was indeed the mouth of a winding canyon through which two small streams frothed down the canyon's steeply pitched floor, at the base of both steep walls.

"We'll rest and switch horses here," Longarm said, stepping down from his saddle.

"Do you ever get tired of giving orders?" Miss Pritchard asked grouchily as she walked her own mount up next to his, leading the spare by its bridle reins. The third dead killer's horse was still trailing them, afraid to be left behind, which was all right with Longarm. The spare was keeping up, staying close; he and the girl might need the rangy cream in a pinch.

Longarm looked at the girl. She looked wind- and sunburned, and her hair was a mess. A pretty mess, but a mess just the same. He didn't blame her for being in a bad mood, and he felt a little guilty for being hard on her before, so he merely said, "I'll take a look around, make sure no one's close."

"You do that."

When he returned twenty minutes later, he was surprised to see that she'd built a fire and set coffee to boil. She'd also laid out a small pouch of jerky and some leftover rabbit. She sat back against a rock, her knees up, nibbling the jerky and sipping from a steaming tin cup.

Longarm walked over and squatted beside the fire. She'd set a cup out for him. He glanced at her. She looked away as she chewed, pointedly ignoring him. He picked up the cup as well as a leather swatch and reached for the coffeepot.

He'd only just touched the handle when a shot sounded—sharp and flat, like a slap against the sky.

The slug tore the coffeepot out of Longarm's hands with an angry clang. The girl screamed.

Chapter 11

Longarm snaked his right hand across his belly for his Colt.

"I wouldn't do that."

The man's voice came from behind him. As Longarm's hand froze on the polished walnut grips of his .44, he glanced over his right shoulder.

Two men were crouched amongst the rocks about twenty feet up the opposite ridge. Both were bearded and clad in animal furs and skins. One had his Springfield rifle aimed at Longarm. The other, crouched behind a small, square boulder, was grinning idiotically at the girl.

"You bring your pistol up, hoss, I'm gonna have to shoot you," warned the man with the aimed Springfield, in a thick southern accent.

Miss Pritchard sat across the fire from Longarm.

She'd dropped her coffee cup between her legs and now sat with her hands on the ground to either side of her, back ramrod straight. She stared toward the interlopers with her lower jaw hanging, chest rising and falling sharply behind her bulky mackinaw.

"Easy," Longarm told her. "No sudden moves."

"Oh, God . . ." she groaned, as though at the end of her tether.

Longarm straightened and, lifting his hands to his shoulders, palms out, turned slowly toward the two men, both of whom were now carefully making their way down the steep ridge. The man with the rifle—tall and black-bearded and with a weird cast to his right eye—kept the rifle aimed at Longarm as he followed the shorter, quicker man down the ridge.

The little, grinning blond man, who also had a Spencer in his arms though he seemed too preoccupied with the girl to aim it at Longarm, gained the canyon floor first and came stumbling toward the fire. The other man said something too quietly for Longarm to hear, and the little man slowed his shambling pace, moving more consciously as he approached but his light blue eyes holding steady on the girl, lips stretched back from pointed, yellow teeth in a chilling leer.

"Oh, God, oh, God," the girl gasped.

"Shhh." To the men, Longarm said, "I'd offer you a cup of coffee, but you done shot a hole in the pot." He smiled.

The little man stopped about ten feet in front of Longarm and slightly to Longarm's left, regarding the girl like a dog slathering at a bone. The other man came up behind him and stepped to one side. The reason his eye had looked odd from a distance, Longarm saw, was that it was a milky color, probably blind. The knife scar through the brow above it and edging into the cheekbone below it explained the nature of the malady.

Mountain men, possibly prospectors, Longarm thought. They had that wild, paranoid look customary of both occupations. While he was somewhat relieved they were obviously not part of the Babe Younger's vengeance-hungry killers, his relief was tempered by the savagery and depravity in both men's eyes. The little man had an added edge of lunacy.

"That's all right," the big man said, his one good eye on Longarm, "we had some dandelion earlier."

"Dandelion's all right in a pinch," Longarm said. "Personally, I prefer Arbuckles."

"She's purty," said the little blond man, raking his eyes away from Miss Pritchard to grin at the big man to his left.

"Leave her alone here for now, Dawg." To Longarm, the big man said, "What the hell you doin' here? Hardly no one knows about this canyon. This is *our* canyon—Dawg's and mine."

"We're not here to jump your claim," Longarm said. "I'm a federal lawman. I'll show you my badge as long as you don't get jumpy about where I put my hands. The girl's a witness to a murder. We're on the run from the Babe Younger gang."

"Never heard of no Babe Younger."

"Don't doubt it a bit."

The little man said, "Can I have her, Tate?"

The big man looked at Miss Pritchard sitting, horrified, on the other side of the fire. He let his eyes roam across the girl—eyes that had likely not seen a woman in months, maybe years, let alone one as comely as Miss Pritchard even in her bulky, cold-weather attire.

"Yeah, you can have her, Dawg. We can both have her. But not yet." He returned his look to Longarm and licked his lips. "Mister, you turn around and get down on your hands and knees."

Longarm shook his head.

"You hear me?" the big man raged, aiming his rifle at Longarm's head.

"Not gonna happen, Tate. I told you, I'm—"

"I don't care who the hell you are. You could be ol' Moses his ownself, fer all I care. All I know, we need someone to help out in our mine up yonder." The big man glanced at the girl again. "And me an' Dawg need a woman to cook an' clean the cabin, and . . . uh, well, fer a few other things, too." Again, he licked his lips.

Dawg screeched a laugh, showing all those stiletto-shaped, little, yellow teeth in his rotten, black-crusted gums. He jumped up and down on one foot, slapping his hands against his raised other thigh.

"Oh, God," the girl yowled. "You're both *crazy*!"

The little man gave another victorious whoop and lunged toward Miss Pritchard.

"Hold on!"

Longarm grabbed the man's arm. At the same time, he closed his left hand around his pistol's grips. He didn't have the Colt half out of its holster before he saw the big man swing his rifle toward him. Longarm glimpsed the barrel arcing through the air over his head a half second before an aching numbness hammered through his right temple.

All went dark as his knees hit the ground.

Again, the girl screamed.

When the lawman opened his eyes again, he heard someone groan nearby. He blinked against the pain searing his skull and realized it had been himself who had groaned. His head ached miserably, and he had trouble drawing air into his lungs due in no small part to his current position—belly down across his saddle.

He was riding facedown, legs dangling down one side, arms down the other, across the claybank's back. Automatically, he tried to straighten his own back, but he could only lift his arms a few inches. When he tried, he felt a tightening around his ankles.

He narrowed his pain-racked eyes to stare at his wrists, saw the rope binding them and snaking off beneath the clay's belly. The other ends of the rope were obviously tied to his ankles on the other side of the gelding.

He looked to his right. Up past the clay's head, the big man was riding a dun mule, his broad back facing Longarm. In his gloved right hand he held the claybank's bridle reins. To his right, the little man rode a cream mule with a copper-spotted ass. He was leading the girl's coyote dun, the girl sitting upright in the saddle, both her wrists tied to her saddle horn. She still had all her clothes on, and they looked intact, which meant she probably hadn't been treated too badly.

Yet.

To the tails of his and the girl's horses were tied the two spares he'd taken from the killers. A dead mule deer doe was tied over the back of the horse behind Longarm, which meant Tate and Dawg had likely been hunting for meat with which to fill their larder. The third, saddleless horse trotted along behind the group, eager-eyed, still desperate to not be left.

Longarm grunted as he tried to work his wrists free of the ropes. Miss Pritchard turned toward him. Her expression showed her relief that he was still alive and had regained consciousness. It was quickly replaced by a recriminating look before she turned her head back forward, jostling slightly with the sway of her horse.

Frustration bit hard at Longarm as he glanced at both the men ahead of him. Again, he tried to work his wrists free, and again he failed. They were tied good and tight. He turned his attention to his surroundings, wondering where in hell they were.

They seemed to be higher in the mountains now; crusty snow patches and half-melted drifts showed in the forest on the far side of the girl. They were moving along a narrow path through tall spruces and tamaracks from which moss swooped like fish netting. The cool air was rife with the aromatic smell of tree resin and the musk of forest duff.

Squirrels, chipmunks, and birds twittered and chattered around him, one particularly angry squirrel aggravating the throbbing pain in the lawman's head. He gritted his teeth against it, then looked again at the big man leading his horse. From the man's right coat pocket, the walnut grips of his .44 shone.

He glanced behind along the steep, rocky trail.

How far away was the Babe Younger bunch? Obviously, if the gang rode up on Longarm and the girl now, they'd be easy pickings. He felt the sting of the girl's recent look. He'd been a fool for letting himself get taken down and hog-tied by these two cork-headed rock breakers. Somehow, he had to spring himself and the girl.

And he had to do it soon, before they made their plans for the girl come true . . .

They rode for another half hour before the trail flattened out and curved into a clearing abutted on the left by a monolithic chunk of weathered, gray granite that towered a thousand feet from the crown of the forested ridge, its jagged crest raking the clear, cerulean sky. A low-slung, brush-roofed log cabin sat near the base of the ridge. To its right lay a small stable and a pole corral. One mule stood inside the corral, hanging its head over the front gate, flicking its ears and braying as the newcomers moved toward it.

"Look what we got, Edgar!" yelled the little blond man to the mule. "A whole string of fine-lookin' hosses, some rare female flesh, and a big fella to work the diggin's fer us." He grinned at his partner. "While me and

Tate keep the girl busy. Ha! Ain't that right, Tate?"

Both men wheezed with laughter.

As they approached the corral, Miss Pritchard gave Longarm a cold, pitiful look of bald condemnation. He looked at her from under his brows and then let his head sag back down against his stirrup fender, helpless as the proverbial fatted calf.

His and the girl's captors halted their mules in front of the corral gate, and while Edgar and the mules the men were riding brayed raucous greetings, Tate and Dawg stepped down from their saddles.

Longarm seethed with fury but he kept his mouth shut, as well as his eyes, feigning unconsciousness, as the big man walked back to the claybank. He squatted down in front of Longarm.

"Hey, lawman," he said. "You still awake?"

Longarm kept his eyes closed and his body slack.

"Ah, come on—I didn't hit ya that hard!"

Chuckling, Tate stepped back and Longarm heard him slide a knife from a sheath. The man walked around to the other side of the horse and cut Longarm's boots free of the ropes. The lawman slitted his eyes and lifted his head slightly, and watched the crazy blond gent walk over to Miss Pritchard's horse and grin up at her.

He had a knife in his left hand. He set his right hand on her thigh, sort of rubbing it.

"Get your hand off me, you pig!" the girl cried.

"Don't call me no names!" Dawg scolded, pointing an admonishing, gloved finger at her.

Behind Longarm, Tate slapped his rump. "Come on, lawdog. Come on down from there."

Longarm kept his head down, his eyes closed.

As Dawg continued to reprimand Miss Pritchard while slicing through her ropes with his knife, Tate reached up the back of Longarm's coat, grabbed the lawman by his waistband and cartridge belt, and tugged him down the horse's left hip. Longarm rolled fluidly off the horse and hit the ground on his side, groaning now as he pretended to awaken from his stupor.

On the other side of his horse, Dawg chuckled lustily. The girl groaned and cried, and there were scuffling sounds. Suddenly, the girl's protestations grew shrill.

"Dawg, damnit—can't you wait till we get her inside?" Tate said.

The man hadn't gotten the last word out of his mouth before Longarm, unable to contain his fury any longer, lifted his head and opened his eyes, scrambling to his feet. He bounded up off his heels and, putting his head down, bulled into Tate, who was half turned away from him, facing his scruffy partner and the girl.

Longarm rammed both shoulders into the man's belly, just below the rifle he'd started swinging around, intending to smash it into Longarm's head. Tate grunted as Longarm picked him up off his feet and drove him straight back into the ground so hard that he could hear the bones in the man's back crack.

The Springfield barked, making Longarm's ears ring. The bullet spanged shrilly off a nearby rock.

Longarm rose from Tate's belly, raised his tied wrists above his head, and smashed them down with savage fury on the man's face, turning his nose sideways against his left, bearded cheek.

"Ohh!" Tate cried as thick blood burst from both nostrils.

"Hey, you dirty devil!" Dawg cried.

His boots thudded as he raced toward Longarm.

The lawman winced, knowing his mistake. He might have put Tate out of commission, but Dawg had him dead to rights. He felt the hair on the back of his head prickle as he waited for the imminent bullet.

Chapter 12

"No!" Miss Pritchard shrieked.

Dawg's Spencer carbine popped behind Longarm. The slug tore a chunk of hard, high-country sod out of the ground to his left.

Dawg screamed, and there was the sharp smack of a gloved hand against flesh. Longarm saw Dawg's shadow move on the ground as he heard the wicked rasp of a cocking lever. He rolled to one side pulling the groaning, bleeding Tate on top of him for a shield.

Smoke and flames stabbed from Dawg's old rifle.

Longarm felt Tate's body convulse as the slug plowed into the big man's chest and exited under his arm, spitting blood into the short, wiry grass beside him. Using both his hands, Longarm dug into the jerking Tate's coat pocket and pulled out his pistol, cocking the hammer back. As Dawg mewled and danced around, staring in wide-eyed shock at his dying partner sprawled back down atop Longarm, the lawman managed to slide out from beneath the big man just far enough to raise the pistol, draw a bead on Dawg, and squeeze the trigger.

The gun roared.

Dawg's lower jaw dropped nearly to his chest as the bullet punched through his brisket, lifting him six inches off the ground and throwing him straight back against Miss Pritchard's coyote dun. The horse side-stepped and whinnied. As Dawg fell to the ground, the horse kicked the crazy blond mountain man in the head with a solid thump.

Dawg rolled onto his side and jerked, kicking his feet like a child having a bitter tantrum, as he died.

Longarm kicked the legs of the dead Tate off of him and rose to his knees. The girl sat back on her heels. She stared at Longarm through the screen of her badly mussed hair. Even through the screen, Longarm could see the blush on her cheek where Dawg had smacked her.

"Are they dead?"

Longarm was breathing heavily as he looked from the big man to Dawg. "Yeah."

He shook his head. The struggle had stirred up the throbbing in his brain plate. He closed his eyes and tried to repress the pain; he had work to do and nearly an entire gang of cutthroats to worry about.

When he opened his eyes again, the girl stood before him, staring up at him, deep lines cutting across her wind-burned forehead. "You look awful."

"I'll be fine in a minute."

"I bet that ride belly down across your saddle didn't do your head any good, did it?" She stepped around beside him, looking at the back of his head. "You got a nice goose egg there. And a gash. We'll need to get that cleaned up."

"More important things to do first."

Longarm walked over to where the big man lay, and with both his tied hands, lifted the man's coat above his cartridge belt from which a sheathed bowie dangled. The girl came over, crouched beside him, and slid the knife from the sheath. Longarm looked at her as, silently, chin down, she carefully sawed the blade through the rope holding his wrists together. The last strand was cut away, and Longarm drew his hands apart and flung away the rope scraps.

"How're you doing?" he asked her.

She drew a deep breath, tossed her hair back away from her face, revealing the sunset-red cheek, and glanced fatefully at the cabin sitting beside the corral, at the base of the monolith-capped ridge. "I reckon I could be worse."

"I reckon we both could."

"What now?"

Longarm straightened and looked around, getting the lay of the place. "I reckon we're about as far up the pass as I intended. Hard way to do it, but we made it. Might as well hole up here."

"Suppose they track us?"

"The trail's too rocky. Only an Injun could track

us up that trace. Oh, they'll find us if they want to bad enough." Longarm stared across the clearing, at where the trail angled in through the forest. "I'm guessing they'll give up by tonight, and start heading down to the low country. Why don't you go on inside and start a fire for coffee? I'll take care of these two and haul our gear in, cut up the deer."

She frowned. "Your head must hurt."

"No more than my pride." Longarm gave a rueful snort, embarrassed about having been taken down by the two rock breakers driven loco by too many lonely winters up here, with nobody but their mules for company.

"I guess I could do that."

When she'd walked over to the cabin, opened the stout timbered door, and disappeared inside, Longarm rubbed the goose egg at the back of his head, then opened the corral gate. He led all the animals inside and unsaddled them, hanging the dressed-out deer from a rope inside the open, lean-to shed on the corral side of the stable, where, judging from the blood on the straw-flecked, hard-packed ground, other such game had been suspended for butchering.

He considered what to do with the two dead men. They could wait. He was too worn out to haul them off until he'd rested and had had a few nips from his bottle. He found a knife amongst the miners' gear in the stable and hacked a haunch off the doe and wrapped it in a burlap feed sack. Hauling it with his saddlebags to the cabin, he looked again toward the south, where the gap in the forest showed where the trail came in.

No movement out that way. No sounds whatever except for birds and tree boughs bending in the breeze. Tate had rung his bell, so he couldn't really trust his judgment until he'd had a few drinks and some food, but he was pretty sure he and the girl were safe here. If the killers found the canyon in which Tate and Dawg had accosted Longarm and the girl, they'd be confused by the extra sets of shod hoofprints, if they could find any amongst the rocks. They might be thrown off the trail altogether.

All Longarm probably had to do now was hole up a few days and make certain that Babe Younger's brigands had gone back to where they'd come from.

The cabin door opened. A cloud of dust and airtight tins flew out the opening, and Longarm heard the snick-snicks of a broom inside. He set the meat and the saddlebags down and, as the sounds of sweeping continued, fetched the rest of his and the girl's gear from the stable. As he approached the cabin again, the girl came out behind another cloud of dust and tins and what appeared a dead mouse, and blew a lock of hair from her eyes.

"It's like a bear den in there." She continued sweeping the refuse out away from the cabin and into the yard. "Go on inside. I have coffee boiling."

"I brought meat."

"Good—I'm hungry. I'll fry us up a couple of steaks."

Longarm looked her over skeptically, vaguely wondering where the frightened, hysterical girl had gone, and where this stalwart homemaker had come from. He grabbed his rifle and the burlap sack with the venison and headed inside, setting both on the table before fetching the rest of the gear inside, as well.

He set his pistol on the table, intending to clean it, and glanced around the shack. It looked tight and sturdy enough. A big fireplace abutted the far right wall. There was a small iron range against the back wall, behind the table of halved pine timbers and chairs crudely constructed from pine logs and braided rawhide.

To the left were two good-sized cots covered with various animal skins. More hides and deer and elk antlers tacked to the walls served as the only decorations. There were no rugs on the knotted puncheon floor badly scuffed and scraped by hobnailed boots. There were a dozen or so shelves built from more halved pine timbers, and they bowed under the weight of an incredible clutter—everything from assaying scales and cyanide bottles to mouse traps and curry combs.

Cobwebbed and molding harnesses hung from spikes. There was a rusty hurricane lamp on the four-by-four center post and, besides a few candles in airtight tins, that appeared all that Longarm and the girl would have for light once the sun had set.

The table was covered with tin cups, plates, food scraps, empty shell casings, ashtrays overflowing with cigar and cigarette butts. As Longarm stood looking around the place, the girl came back inside and cleared the table with two efficient sweeps of her broom, and swept it all out the door and into the yard.

"There."

"You been right busy."

"Coffee?"

"Don't mind if I do."

She leaned the broom against the wall behind the door, where a pick leaned behind several fur coats, then walked over to the range where a black kettle bubbled, sending the smell of coffee into the room that otherwise reeked, as the girl had described the place, of a bear's den. "Have a seat."

Longarm dug his bottle out of his saddlebags and sat down in the chair. He looked across at the girl, who was filling two tin cups with the piping hot brew from the pot. He wasn't sure he should mention it, somehow corrupt it, so he said haltingly, "You . . . seem, uh . . . different."

She set his cup on the table in front of him, set hers on the table's other side. "You mean, I'm no longer screaming?"

Longarm popped the cork on his bottle, splashed some of the tanglefoot into his coffee. "Something like that."

"I don't know what happened," she said, standing and looking down at her cup. "I guess I got tired of being scared. Didn't seem to be working. It was just after those two savages grabbed me."

She jerked her chin toward the open door, toward where Tate and Dawg lay in the grass fronting the corral. "After they hit you, and I thought you were dead until you started groaning as they loaded you onto your horse."

She continued to stare down at her steaming cup. Glancing up at him thoughtfully, she said, "I guess you set a good example, Deputy. You back down to no one, do you? Not even a whole gang of killers. I guess if I were you, I'd have left me where you found me and rode away."

"Well, then," Longarm said, "I reckon you wouldn't have the job very long, would you?"

She smiled at that. He liked the way the gold specks in her green eyes flashed, reflecting the light from the open door behind Longarm. "No, I guess I wouldn't." She looked at him searchingly for several more seconds, and then took a sip of her coffee. "I think I'm tired of being scared."

"Ah, hell—you're tougher than you think you are. If you weren't, you never would have left your home in Pinecone to testify up in Snow Mound against that scurvy devil, Babe Younger."

"No, that was part of my fear, I guess, too." She took another sip of her coffee, set the cup down, and dragged the burlap sack toward her. Opening it, she peered inside, then dragged the haunch out onto the table. "Fear of my employer, Mr. Cable, and my father, the good Reverend Pritchard."

"Afraid I don't quite understand, Miss Pritchard. They pressured you into traveling up to Snow Mound?"

"In their own ways." Squatting near the range, she was rummaging around in a low cupboard full of cooking utensils. She returned to the table with a skinning knife. She set it down beside the haunch, and a troubled look stole across her face. "Me and Mr. Cable, you see . . . We have more than just a business relationship."

"Ah."

"Yes." She drew a deep breath, and let it out slowly. "I have no feelings for the man, and I doubt he has any feelings for me. If he did, he probably wouldn't have sent me to Snow Mound with only two Pinkertons to protect me. Wouldn't he have come himself?"

She looked at Longarm as though expecting an answer to her question.

"A good man would have accompanied you, yeah. He wouldn't have sent you alone, even if he had hired a couple of bodyguards."

"Yes. They were just to lessen his guilt." Color rose in her cheeks as she took up the knife and began carving away at the haunch. "My father, the good reverend, is no better. Mr. Cable built his church, holds the sizeable note on it."

"He didn't join you, either."

She pressed her lips together as she carved a steak from the haunch, deftly avoiding the gristle and choosing the tenderest parts of the meat. "I went not so much out of fear, I guess, but because I'm weak. You saw it yourself in the hotel room. A frightened little child, afraid of her own shadow . . . or the man she sleeps with to keep her job, and of the man who pretends not to know I'm sleeping with Mr. Cable but secretly approves. Because he's weak, too." Her left hand shook as she set aside the steak she'd just carved. "I guess all we Pritchards are weak, Mr. Long."

"Both Mr. Cable and the good reverend would be quaking in their boots, if they found themselves in this situation."

She laughed. It was really more of a delighted sigh, as though she were imagining how either man would react to being here in this veritable bear's den. Also an expression of her relief at having found more steel in herself than either man could ever hope of finding.

Longarm sipped his coffee. He turned the cup in a slow, thoughtful circle on the table. "You know what I'd do once you get back to Pinecone?"

She was holding the deer's dun-and-cream hide back while she carved the steak out from under it, slicing through the silk-thin layer of pale fat coating the liver-colored venison. "What's that?"

"I'd tell both men to go to hell."

Again, she smiled as she continued to cut. "You would at that. And I just might, too. If I still feel as brave . . . or as strong . . . as I do now. With you here," she added, looking at him. She thought of something. "Look at me—I've been so wrapped up in myself I completely forgot about you."

She looked around, finally grabbed a ragged scrap of towel, and went out the back door. He heard her walking around back there, her footsteps fading before growing louder as she returned. She came back into the cabin holding the cloth closed around a lump in her hands.

"There's still some snow back there. Here." She handed it over to the table to him. "Press that to your head. Bring the swelling down."

"Obliged." Longarm held the pack to the top of his head, wincing a little at the ache that quickly subsided after the snow's initial cold shock.

"You know what I think, Miss Pritchard, since we seem to be getting along better now . . . ?"

She stepped back and arched a brow, a slight flush rising in her tapering cheeks. "What's that, Deputy?"

He turned his chair around, so that he could see out the door and across the clearing. "I think you oughta call me Longarm." He glanced over his shoulder and winked at her. "Most folks do."

Those gold flecks flashed again as she smiled. "Then you may call me Jo. I know it's not a very attractive handle, Longarm, but it's the only one I have."

"You make it just about as pretty a name as I ever heard, Jo," Longarm said.

She blushed and turned to the stove. As she added more wood to the firebox and began frying the venison steaks, Longarm sipped his coffee and stared out the open door, keeping an eye out for the Babe Younger cutthroats.

He was likely wasting his time.

The gang was probably headed for Utah by now . . .

Chapter 13

Longarm adjusted the focus on his government-issue field glasses, and the black speck clarified and grew in size as it swooped low over a sprawling pine. He saw the raptor's white head and tail, long, yellow beak, predatory eyes, and the flinty, granite-black feathers rippling in the late-afternoon wind.

The golden sunshine flashed silver off the bird's sleek back. The yellow talons folded down from the long body. The broad, ragged wings rose, and the toes hooked over the edge of the barrel-sized nest of woven brush, branches, and pine needles.

From the bald eagle's beak drooped a silver fish, just now flicking its tail. The big raptor dropped the fish into the nest amongst five of its fuzzy, charcoal-colored offspring. Longarm watched as the big raptor tore bits of meat from the fish and fed each of her offspring in turn, dropping the ragged chunks of flesh into each waiting, upturned mouth. Then she rose up out of the nest once more, becoming airborne with the heavy flapping of her powerful wings. Behind, all five fuzzy heads with big, perpetually open, black beaks dropped down to feed on what was left of the trout the mother bird had likely pulled from a lake or river that Longarm could not see from his vantage point.

He slid the lenses to the right, raking the pine forest southwest, to a far, rocky ridge, then pulled them down a little to inspect the trail twisting up from the canyon about two miles below and southeast—the trail up which Tate and Dawg had hauled him and the girl.

No movement on the trail. He scouted several clearings on either side of it, and saw nothing there, either, except a few mule deer sunning themselves in the greening spring grass of a gentle slope.

Now he slid the glasses to his left, following the trail through the forest and into the clearing where the cabin sat at the base of the giant knob of weathered granite turning slate gray as the sun angled behind it and began stretching purple shadows across the clearing. Smoke rose from the stone hearth.

Longarm had saddled his claybank and rode up here, on this knob jutting out from the main ridge, to scout the area around the cabin. He hadn't come far, because he hadn't wanted to leave Jo Pritchard alone for long in the cabin. From here he had a good view of all the possible routes the killers might take on their way up the ridge from below.

Up higher and behind him, the wind was blowing. It sounded like a distant train under a full head of steam. But down here, lower on the knob, all was quiet. Except for the slightly bending pine crowns below and him, all was still.

Maybe it was all too still and too quiet. He wasn't sure. But for some reason, he felt a prickle of apprehension deep in his belly. Probably just his old instincts telling him not to let his guard down. Just when he thought that he and the girl had outrun the killers, they'd likely show.

On the other hand, maybe, as he'd thought might happen, they'd indeed grown bored with the hunt for the girl—after all, killing her wasn't going to bring Babe up out of his cold grave—and had moved on to the wreaking of more havoc elsewhere. He hoped so.

Satisfied that no one was skulking around out here at the moment, and with night falling fast, they likely wouldn't be for a while, Longarm grabbed his rifle and picked his way down off the escarpment and into the hollow in which the clay was tied. He slid the Winchester into its saddle boot, returned the field glasses to their scratched case, and dropped them into a saddle-bag pouch.

Stepping into the saddle, he threaded his way through the escarpments, then rode on down the mountain, crossed the trail, and entered the clearing in which the cabin sat, thick smoke pouring from its chimney. Jo must have stoked the stove against the coming chill.

Longarm returned the clay to its stable, where he unsaddled the mount and forked hay to it and the others. He hauled water from the creek that snaked around behind the cabin and stable, filling the stock trough, then headed back to the cabin.

He wrapped his hand around the front door knob and pushed the door open a foot. Inside, Jo, sitting in a washtub filled with soapy water, her blond hair piled atop her beautiful head, gasped and covered her wet, soapy breasts with her arm. Longarm felt a sting of automatic lust as he saw her close her right hand over her right, tender breast, but closed the door only about a second after he'd opened it.

"Sorry, Jo! I didn't know you were bathing!" he said through the door.

"I'll be done in a minute, Longarm," the girl called, the fear gone from her voice. Again, she called from inside the cabin. "Sorry—I decided to heat water for a bath just after you left."

"No problem." Longarm turned away from the door as though from the remembered image of her sitting there in the tub that did nothing to hide her firm, young, pink-tipped breasts adorned with diaphanous soap bubbles. "No problem at all," he added wryly, sitting down on a log bench fronting the cabin and digging a nickel cheroot from his shirt pocket.

He tried to keep his mind off the girl, remembering Billy Vail's admonishment cloaked as a joke. It would be damned unprofessional as well as downright careless of him to try to bed the girl out here, with a whole gang of cutthroats possibly on their heels. But his pecker tingled as he sat there, firing the cheroot and listening to the water splashing on the other side of the door.

"Longarm?" she called after a time. "Would you come in here, please?"

Longarm groaned against the tightness of his pants as he rose from the bench and, clamping the cigar between his teeth, opened the cabin door. The girl stood at the range atop which two kettles of water steamed. "Would you empty my bathwater?" Facing the water steaming on the range, she smiled at him over her shoulder exposed by the overlarge, man's wool shirt hanging off of it. "If you'll haul water from the creek, I'll fix you up your own nice, hot bath. Hot water's almost ready."

Longarm looked at her—even in the men's overlarge duds, she was one delightful, alluring display of female curves—and rolled the cigar between his lips. "Ah, you don't need to do that, Miss Jo."

"Oh, it feels so good to get the trail grime off, Longarm. I insist!" She grinned at him—coquettishly? "Go on now. It won't take a minute, and then I'll fry us up some more steaks for supper. I even found some beans and greens in airtight tins!"

"Oh, well . . . hell."

Longarm rolled the cigar from one corner of his mouth to the other as he picked up the tub by its metal handles and hauled it out the back door and emptied it into the brush. He went back into the cabin, set down the tub, and picked up a wooden bucket by the door, letting his eyes rake the girl's small, curvy frame once more as she rummaged around on a high shelf near the range, rising onto the toes of her black boots.

The jeans she wore were much too large for her, but they still revealed a nicely rounded ass and gently curving hips tapering to well-turned thighs.

"Knock it off, you cork-headed fool," he grumbled silently to himself as he carried the bucket out toward the stream flashing beyond a screen of willows dappled with late-afternoon salmon light. "You're supposed to be protecting the girl, not *fucking* her!"

Well, taking a bath wasn't fucking her. He could think about fucking her, though, couldn't he? As good as she looked, what man wouldn't be entertaining such thoughts?

When he returned to the cabin, she was pouring one of the kettles of hot water into the washtub. Steam wafted above the tub and into the shadowy air of the cabin.

"What're you gonna do while I bathe?"

"Don't worry," she said, removing the second steam pot from the range. "I won't peek."

She gave him a coy, little smile, then dumped the water into the tub. Longarm set his own bucket down, then sagged into a kitchen chair.

"I'll sit right here," she said, turning a chair out away from the opposite side of the table, facing the front window right of the door. "I'll keep watch while you wash."

Longarm looked at her, one brow arched skeptically.

She glanced at him over her shoulder, ran her eyes up and down his brawny frame. "You're not modest, are you, Marshal?"

Longarm kicked out of his left boot. "I wouldn't call it modest. I'd call it . . . prudent, I reckon. Professional maybe's more the word."

"Whatever do you mean, Marshal?"

"I mean, takin' my clothes off in a cabin out in the middle of nowhere with a pretty girl ain't what some might call professional."

"Oh, I don't know. I don't think there's anything unprofessional about cleaning oneself. Go ahead, now. Don't be shy. You get cleaned up and I'll keep watch out the window. I have a feeling you're right, though, and the gang's long gone from here by now."

"I hope we're both right," Longarm said, glancing at the girl to make sure she had her head turned away, then rose from his chair.

He glanced at her again. She was looking out the window, her legs crossed, hands in her lap. She still had her hair pinned up, exposing the pale back of her neck, the flesh soft and ripe for kissing. Silently admonishing himself, and wincing at the continued tightening across his upper pants legs, he shucked out of his coat, hung it on an elk antler nailed to the wall, then pulled his shirttails out of his tobacco tweed slacks.

"Don't look, now," he admonished the girl. "Wouldn't be . . . well, professional . . . for you to go seein' me in my birthday suit."

Not only that, but he was embarrassed about his hard-on.

"It would only be getting you back," she said, teasing.

"How's that?"

She turned her head slightly. "You saw me in mine."

"Don't look, dang it!" he scolded her.

She laughed and turned her head away. "That was an accident," Longarm said as he shrugged out of his shirt and hung it, too, on the elk antlers.

As he unbuttoned his suddenly too-tight trousers and slid them down his legs, she said with that same air of good-natured teasing, "I noticed you didn't pull the door closed very quickly, Longarm."

"I pulled it closed just as quick as I could. I'm a professional, Miss Jo, and it's important we keep that straight. I'm here to protect you, see you home safely."

"I couldn't agree more," she said, and he glanced back to see her cheek pulled back slightly as she sat there, staring out the window and smiling.

Longarm hung his longhandles on the elk antlers, and, as naked as the day he was born and scared as hell she was going to turn around and see him here, his cock at half-mast despite his silent pleas for it to play fair, he added hot water to the cold until he had the bath temperature about one degree above what would sear off three layers of skin and stepped into the tub.

As he crouched, placing his hands on the tub's edges, he glanced over his shoulder to make sure the girl was still facing away from him. She was. And she was still smiling that annoying smile that for some reason was keeping his cock at half-mast and threatening to go higher.

"Saw a family of eagles," he said by way of distracting conversation, as he sank down into the eight inches of wonderfully hot and steaming water. Gooseflesh rose on his shoulders and across the back of his neck. "Leastways, a mother and five little ones. Ugly little things, baby eagles. In a cute sort of way."

"Oh, I wish I could have seen!"

"Maybe we'll both ride out there tomorrow."

"That'd be fun. A nice distraction from all this."

Longarm snagged the cake of soap and a rag scrap off the chair near the tub, where the girl had left them with a towel she must have packed in her carpetbags. He soaked and lathered the rag, and began raking it across his chest.

"She was feeding the little ones a fish, taking little bites out of it and dropping them into their gaping beaks." Longarm chuckled, casting another cautious glance over his shoulder, pleased to see the girl still facing away from him.

Deciding the faster he scrubbed himself and climbed out of the tub the better, he scrubbed his face and the back of his neck and then rose to a crouch to scour both legs and feet and to clean his privates. He dropped back down into the tub and splashed himself, rinsing himself off.

"Good enough," he said, reaching for the towel draped over the back of the chair.

He felt something against the back of his neck. In his ear, she said quietly, "You haven't washed your back yet, Longarm." He jumped with a start. "Want me to help?"

"Now, damnit," he complained, "you promised to sit over there in your chair and stare out the damn window!"

"I'm just trying to help!"

"Ah, hell!"

"Give me the rag, and stop acting like a child. You saw my breasts, and I know you enjoyed seeing them. It's only right I get a little look at you . . . which, um . . ." She giggled in his other ear. "Isn't so little at all!"

"Ignore that damn thing—it has a mind of its own." Longarm slapped the soap into her open palm. "If you're gonna scrub, scrub. Be quick about it, so I can get out of here. Damn unprofessional, is what this is."

"How 'bout this?" she said in a sexy-raspy voice, so close to his ear that he could feel her hot breath. She reached into the tub and wrapped her hand around his cock. "Would the powers that be consider this unprofessional, too?"

She pumped him slowly.

Chapter 14

Longarm groaned as the girl, her delicate, long-fingered hand wrapped around his piston-hard staff, pumped him once more.

Longarm's eyes grew heavy and slid slowly down over his eyes. "Oh . . . that ain't nice, Miss Jo . . ."

The girl tittered as she ran her hand very slowly up from the bottom of his cock, her hand making wet sounds against his skin. "I think you like it."

"Just the back'll do."

"What's that? I couldn't hear you."

"I said . . . I'll thank you to just scrub my back."

"Oh." Jo removed her hand from his cock, leaving it to stand there at full, throbbing mast between his legs. "All right. Your back it is," she said with a sigh of feigned resignation.

As she rinsed the rag out in the water near his cock

and balls, he could feel her penetrating eyes on the side of his face. He watched her hands, fascinated, lust stabbing through him from bowels to throat, constricting his breathing. She ran the soap over the rag, set the soap onto the chair.

"Lean forward," she ordered him.

He did as he was told, and she raked the rag across his broad shoulders. She scrubbed hard, and he could hear her grunting softly as she worked, working the rag across his skin from the back of his neck down to the small of his back.

It was a wonderful feeling—having all those tight muscles worked, getting all that trail grime off. A sweet, luxurious feeling. When she was finished, unable to help himself, unable to keep his raging need for the girl on its leash any longer, he reached back, wrapped his hand around her arm, and drew her to the tub's right side.

"What is it, Longarm?" she asked quietly, throatily.

Her lips parted. They were dark pink and etched with very tiny vertical lines. Her skin was as smooth as a baby's bottom. Her green eyes danced with gold dust while strands of her honey-blond hair curled down over her forehead and brushed the sides of her face.

"I think I'm gonna kiss you, Miss Jo."

"I'd like nothing better, Longarm."

"And then I'm going to enjoy your body, but with the understanding it's damn . . ."

"I know," she said, sliding her face up close to his, taking his head in her hands and gently tugging on his ears. "Damned unprofessional." She kissed his chin. "Don't worry—it'll be our secret."

He tightened his grip on her arms, drew her closer, and closed his mouth over hers. They kissed gently for a time while Longarm sat there in the tub, and then, as their body temperatures rose and they each started quivering slightly with desire, and their heartbeats quickened, they entangled their tongues and ran their hands desperately across each other's bodies—feeling, grasping, working, kneading.

Finally, Longarm rose from the tub, water cascading off his long, broad, brown body, and reached for the towel.

The girl grabbed it first. "Let me," she said.

Remaining on her knees beside the tub, she began running the towel, which was damp from her own bath, across his left hip and down his left thigh. While she did, she held her face within two inches of the large, mushroom head of the big lawman's throbbing member.

"That is some cock you have, Longarm." She looked up at him from beneath her thin, blond brows. "Do you think me depraved for saying so?"

"Not at all," he croaked.

While she dried his other leg, she leaned forward and touched the end of her tongue to the tip of his cock.

Longarm drew a shallow breath.

She looked up at him, smiling. "I can't wait to get that inside me." She caressed it again with her tongue, then drew her tongue back into her ripe mouth, and swallowed. "I've only been with two men in my life—one being Mr. Cable." She shook her head as she inspected the large, throbbing cock before her. "Never even seen one that size!"

She closed her mouth over the head of it and groaned as she sucked, making her cheeks bulge. She turned her head from one side to the other, groaning and sucking and running her wet tongue across his cock, slathering and sucking and making little gagging sounds when she drew the head too far down her throat.

Longarm opened his mouth to draw a deep blast of air into his lungs, rocking back on his heels in the tub.

She made another gagging sound, then drew her mouth back off of him, spittle webbing from her moist lower lip to the head of his raging hard-on. "Am I doing it right? I've never done it before. Always wanted to, but I reckon I didn't know the right man."

Her smile dimpled her cheeks.

"You're goin' at it like a pro," he said around the frog in his throat.

She was about to slide her lips over him once more when he sandwiched her head in his hands and held her back. "Time to do this good and proper."

He grabbed the towel off the chair and stepped out of the tub. She rose and stepped back, quickly unbuttoning her shirt. She watched him as he dried himself. He stared at her, watched in sublime fascination as she removed the big shirt, dropped it to the floor, and then lifted her chemise over her head, dropping it onto the shirt. Her breasts were large and ripe, the pink nipples jutting like spring rosebuds ready to burst. One was ever so slightly larger than the other.

He dropped the towel and stood watching her kick out of her boots and shuck out of the rest of her clothes until she stood naked before him, her hair hanging in a beguiling tangle around her face. She held her chin down and stared at him, her green eyes dark with need.

As though an unseen hand reached out from reality to touch his shoulder, reminding him of the possible danger, he glanced out the window. The clearing was filled with shadows. Night was falling quickly. Nothing moved except a single mountain jay that had perched on the windowsill and was tilting its pointed-beaked head from side to side, as though deeply interested in what was happening on the other side of the glass.

Jo laughed. "He thinks we're fascinating."

Longarm moved to her, raked his fingers lightly across her shoulders. "He's about to get a show."

She drew a deep breath through parted lips.

Longarm kissed her hard and passionately. After a time, while she stroked him with both hands, he crouched and sucked each nipple in turn, until both were hard as stones and her breasts were rising and falling heavily as she breathed.

Finally, Longarm placed his hands on her shoulders, turned her gently toward the table. He spread her legs about shoulder-width apart, stuck his hands between her legs, and fingered her damp, silky nest.

"Oh!" Her hair flying, she bent forward against the table.

"Are you ready?" Longarm asked her, sticking two fingers between the petallike folds, poking and prodding and causing her to moan and sigh.

"Never . . . been . . . readier . . . ! Oh, Jesus, fuck me, Longarm!"

"I oughta be ashamed of myself," he said, glancing out the window on the table's other side, making sure the clearing was still empty. "But I reckon we've come too far to turn back now."

He used his hand to guide his cock between her legs and into the pink slit waiting for him beneath her partially spread buttocks. As soon as the mushroom head disappeared, she lifted her head and arms and clamped her hands over the far edge of the table.

"Oh . . . God . . . that feels good!"

Longarm grunted, drawing his lips back from his teeth as he spread his feet on the splintery floor and slowly shoved the entire length of his rod inside the girl's womb. As he did so, she arched her back tighter and tighter and gripped the table harder and harder, groaning as though she were being slowly run through with a bayonet.

"Oh, fuck . . . oh, fuck . . . that feels soooo fucking *good*!"

"Such farm talk," Longarm chastised the girl as he hit bottom and, feeling her sweet, hot snatch convulsing around him, began sliding back out.

"Yes," she said, wagging her ass, "the good reverend wouldn't approve. Well, fuck him!" she cried. "Fuck them all!"

Longarm chuckled and rammed himself hard inside her. She threw her head back and mewled as though in the throes of death, and then lowered her head once more as he started withdrawing again.

When he'd pulled out the third time, he began hammering against her, harder and harder and with the regularity of a ticking clock—over and over, over and over, making the table lurch loudly back and forth across the floorboards, and evoking piercing love howls and coyote-like yammers from deep in the girl's bosom.

As he toiled, Longarm reached around her and cupped her flopping breasts in his hands. She released her own right hand from the table and mashed it hard over his right hand against her breast, and swore as he continued ramming himself deep inside her.

They came together in a cataclysm of hot, naked, sweating flesh, love cries, and jetting fluid. When their joint screams had died, Jo flopped breast down against the table, and for a moment he thought she'd stopped breathing. Then her sides expanded as she drew a breath, and he lifted her, turned her around, and kissed her.

She snaked her arms around his neck and clung to him, returning his kiss and mashing her breasts against his chest.

"Oh, God," she groaned when he stopped to scoop her up in his arms and carry her over to one of the two cots on the room's far side. He laid her onto the furs, then walked over to the hearth and chunked several more logs on the fire.

Brushing his hands across his thighs, his dong still at half-mast and swinging back and forth, half slumbering, he strode to the window and looked out. Nothing. He opened the door and walked out onto the worn area in the ground fronting the cabin. The stove, steam, fireplace, and heat of his and Jo's passion had stoked a fire inside him, and the cooling night air felt good sliding against him.

The breeze smelled like pine. Smoke from the chimney hearth slithered down over the roof and flitted away on the breeze stealing over the granite crest of the mountain.

"Longarm!"

He bolted back inside the cabin, half expecting to see an unshaven brigand grabbing Jo and holding a knife to her throat. "What the hell is it?"

She rolled over on the cot to face him with an enticing grin. "That was fun. Will you do me again?"

"Christ, girl," he said, closing the door. "Thought ole Babe Younger's boys had ya."

"Nah." She giggled and lowered her eyes to his cock. "Just horny!"

Longarm chuckled, picked up his gun and shell belt, and returned to the cot. He coiled the rig around the right post at the front of the cot, so that the .44's handle was within easy reach if he should need it. Sagging down beside the girl, he kissed her while she stroked him back to life again, pulling at his cock, massaging his balls.

When he was fully erect and could feel his blood

washing in his ears, he positioned himself between her legs, which she spread as wide as she could and made little grunting sounds as she scuttled down lower on the cot and dug her heels into the backs of his legs.

"Fuck me," she whispered, running a hand down his unshaven jaw. "Fuck me one more time, and I'll never ask you for another thing."

Longarm fucked her slow and easy at first, taking his time. After about ten minutes of this, the cot creaking gently beneath them, he rose up on his outstretched arms and his toes, and drove her hard.

She mewled beneath him, panting and grunting and flopping her knees and digging her heels into his legs, occasionally lifting her head to close her mouth over his shoulder. He was nearly to his climax—thrusting, withdrawing, and thrusting again—when he saw a shadow move in the front window to the right of the door.

His loins heaved deliciously, and he exploded inside the girl, who lifted her head and loosed an ear-rattling shriek as she bucked up against him.

Longarm looked at the front door. The metal knob turned slowly.

Unable to stop to save his life, Longarm reached forward and, as he continued pumping, his seed jettisoning into the screaming girl, he slid his Colt from its holster.

The front door slammed inward with a bang. A coated, bearded figure bolted into the cabin.

Longarm extended the Colt straight out from the

bed and fired twice, the blasts sounding like cannon fire in the tight confines. As the man there screamed and spun back out the opening, the back door blew open and another man ran into the cabin, raising a carbine and aiming toward the bed.

The Colt leaped and roared twice more in Longarm's hands. The second shooter flew back against the wall, firing his carbine into the ceiling before piling up at the base of the range, blood oozing from the two holes in his forehead.

Longarm lowered the smoking pistol, rose up on his toes, and finished flooding the girl with his hot jism.

She stared up at him, wide-eyed, laughing hysterically, believing, it seemed, that the shooting had been merely to celebrate his and the girl's simultaneous fulfillment.

Chapter 15

Longarm dragged the second man he'd shot through the brush lining the creek. He had the man's ankles clamped under his arms. He trudged forward through the thick brush, dragging the man behind him.

When he came to the place to which he'd dragged the first man, he dropped the second dead man's feet without ceremony. The man's boots thudded to the ground, crunching last year's dead leaves.

He backed away from the cadavers, who lay staring upward, both men's mouths still stretched in the same grimaces they'd worn when Longarm's bullets had slammed through them. The lawman dropped to a knee, looking around and listening, his breath frosting in the air before him.

The stars winked sharply overhead—more sharply in the east than in the west, where the sun had dropped only about an hour ago. A coyote howled in the toothy, rocky ridges rising in the north. There was a slight breeze that made the willow limbs scratch together and the new leaves flutter, and the stream chuckled quietly over its stony bed.

Otherwise, it was quiet out here.

No unnatural sounds, anyway.

Longarm rolled a cold cheroot from one side of his mouth to the other as he continued to look around. Were these two the only two gang members out here? Or were there more? These two might have scouted the clearing alone, but others might have heard the shots, which would have carried far and wide on such a quiet night here in this natural amphitheater formed by the large block of granite looming from atop the western ridge.

Others might have come and be out here now. Or be on their way.

No way of telling.

Longarm cursed and bit the end of the cold cheroot angrily. He'd been wrong about the Younger bunch growing bored with stalking the girl and hightailing it back to wherever they'd come from. Deep down, he'd known it was a long shot, or at least a medium-long shot. Men like that didn't give up easily once they'd set out on a mission. Also, they'd see the killing of the girl for testifying against their leader as a matter of pride.

The only good thing about Longarm's and the girl's situation now was that he'd managed to whittle the gang down by five over the past two days. That left eight, if he'd counted correctly. Long odds, but better than they'd been. He'd been up against eight before.

He remained there on a knee, looking around and listening, for nearly ten minutes. Finally, when he'd heard nothing that seemed out of sorts, he rose and walked a few yards out of the trees, hugging the creek, as he made his way slowly over to the stable and corral. He checked on the horses, then continued tramping north away from the cabin, all his senses alert.

He spent another ten minutes at the far edge of the clearing, where the stony slope rose toward the northern ridge, scrutinizing every rock and shadow, his brain keen to even the slightest leaf rustle or the soft thud of a cone tumbling from a pine.

He traced a broad circle back toward the cabin, cutting across the center of the clearing, ready to drop and fire his .44 at the slightest shadow movement, click of a gun hammer, or crunch of a grass blade. Seeing or hearing no one, he returned to the cabin, tapped quietly on the door with two knuckles.

"Jo?" he said just above a whisper, looking across the dark, star-shrouded clearing behind him. "It's me."

He heard the scrape of the locking bar being lifted from its metal brackets. The latch clicked, and the girl pulled the door open, stepping back, her eyes wide in the starlight. Longarm stepped inside, closed the door quickly, and returned the locking bar to its brackets.

"Anything?" Jo said, keeping her voice low. She held Longarm's rifle in her arms across her chest.

He shook his head. "Got a feelin' the gang had split

up to scour the pass. Likely, the others heard the shots, though. We'll have to assume they did."

Jo nodded, set the rifle across a chair, and sat down at the table upon which Longarm had laid out all his spare pistols and ammo. The coffeepot stood at the end of the table. She glanced at it. "Would you like a shot?"

"I reckon." Longarm looked around, wondering if there was any way to make the cabin more secure than he'd already made it by closing and latching the shutters over all the windows and barring both doors. They had a fire popping in the hearth, and another one made the range tick.

Jo filled a coffee cup and slid it across the table. Longarm sagged down in the chair, picked up the cup, and looked through the steam rising from it. Jo closed her upper lip over the rim of her own tin cup.

"How you doin'?" he asked her.

She sipped from the cup, swallowed, and glanced at the pistol. "Scared as hell." She hardened her eyes. "But if they get me, I'm gonna go down shooting."

Longarm smiled and reached across the table to take one of her hands in his and squeeze it affectionately. "Mr. Cable's not gonna recognize you."

She returned his smile. It faded quickly under an expression of concern. "No more out there, though, huh?"

"I don't think so. If they were, they would have showed themselves by now." Longarm scratched a match to life on the scarred surface of the table. Lighting the cheroot and puffing smoke, he said out one corner of his mouth, "We could pull out of here, head deeper into the mountains. But I'm inclined to hole up here."

He blew the match out with a puff of smoke, tossed it onto the floor, and drew a bracing lungful of the pungent tobacco. "The cabin's sturdy enough, and might be as secure as any cover we'd find out there. They might try to burn us out, but they'll have trouble getting a torch onto the roof with us returning fire from the windows."

"I guess we just watch and wait, huh?"

Longarm sipped his coffee, nodding.

"Those two human grizzlies who lived here had a good store of coffee beans, anyway. I'll keep a pot going."

"Good—we'll need it." Longarm looked at her. "Why don't you crawl back into bed? You could do with some shut-eye."

She shook her head. "Too keyed up, I reckon." She stared down at the steaming cup she held between her hands and cleared her throat. "I just want you to know, Longarm—I wouldn't want to be holed up in a tight spot like this with anyone but you."

Her eyes grew soft, and a smile touched her mouth corners.

"Me, too, Miss Jo."

She canted her head to one side, speculatively. "You got a girl at home, Longarm?"

The lawman glanced down at the copper moon-and-star badge pinned to his coat. "Just this one here. Besides, I'm fun in the short run but tiresome outside of a few days. You'll see."

"I hope so," she said with a sigh. "More coffee?"

"Don't mind if I do."

They drank coffee for a time, mostly in silence, waiting, listening.

The night deepened, chilly air pushing through the rough chinking between the cabin's logs. After Jo grew sleepy and decided to lie down for a while, Longarm turned the lantern low and kept the fire built up. He sat in a chair with his back to the door, holding his rifle across his thighs, ears pricked though the only sounds he heard were the occasional breeze, the infrequent scuttle of a night bird pecking at the sod on the roof, and the sporadic, thin, distant cries of coyotes and wolves.

He dozed for a time, then lifted his chin from his chest suddenly, squeezing the rifle in his hands. He frowned, looked down at his gloved hands on the rifle, wondered what had awakened him and why his heartbeat had quickened slightly.

Had he heard something?

He looked at Jo, who slept beneath the skins on the bed. Her blond hair shone like honey in the faint light emanating from the lamp. Her shoulders rose and fell deeply as she slept. Likely, it wasn't her who had awakened Longarm.

He rose from the chair, wincing as the old, dry wood creaked beneath him, then walked quietly over to the back door. Holding the rifle across his belly, he tipped his head to the door, listening.

Nothing.

He removed the locking bar, leaned it gently against the wall, then unlatched the door and stepped outside, quietly closing the door behind him, stepping to one side, and sitting down with his back against the cabin. Here, his shadow would blend with that of the shack.

He stared through the screen of trees and brush toward the creek, a rippling silver sheen running along the base of the western ridge. The night was still, but the threads of isolated breezes ruffled the willows' uppermost branches. The air smelled fresh, cold, and loamy. Longarm frowned as he worked his nostrils. On the chill air was also, faintly, fleetingly, the smell of cigarette smoke.

He continued to sniff the breeze as he tried to find the direction from which the smoke, which he could now no longer smell, had emanated. From the other side of the creek, possibly. From the north.

His pulse quickened once more as he gained his feet and stole quickly through the brush to the creek. A downed tree provided a ford. He crossed it on the balls of his feet. He was almost to the opposite side when his right foot slid off the wet log and made a dull plop as it hit the shallow water.

Stopping, he dropped to a knee, raised his rifle high across his chest, and looked around, awaiting a rifle flash and possible bullet. When none came, he sniffed the breeze, and after a few seconds, with the cool air pressing against his face, he detected the fleeting scent of tobacco smoke. It seemed to just graze his nose and

disappear. But it was definitely coming from upstream
somewhere; the breeze was out of that direction.

Longarm walked ahead along the stream that mur-
mured to his right. The boulder- and cedar-stippled
ridge was on his left. He kept an eye out for the glow
of a cigarette, but whoever was out here wouldn't be
stupid enough to not at least conceal the coal, would
he?

One step at a time, Longarm walked, holding the
Winchester straight up and down in front of him. When
he'd walked maybe ten yards, he caught the smoke
scent again for about half a second before it disappeared.

He'd just passed a thumb of rock jutting from the
base of the ridge when a pebble rattled down off the
top of the scarp to his left. A cigarette butt followed it,
sparking.

Longarm wheeled. Before him, standing atop the
thumb, a man's shadow was raising a rifle. The Winchester leaped and roared twice in the lawman's hands,
both shell casings clattering onto the ground around his
boots. The man fired his own rifle between Longarm's
staccato shots, and the slug spanged off a rock somewhere near the creek upstream from the lawman.

The man atop the escarpment wheezed and raised
his rifle barrel as he awkwardly levered a fresh round
into the chamber. Longarm fired twice more quickly,
and watched the man fall back off the thumb, heard the
rifle clatter off the rocks.

Another rifle cracked upstream from Longarm. The

slug tore into the side of the escarpment as he wheeled and dove behind a boulder half in and half out of the creek. Edging a look around the boulder, he saw a flash. The gun screamed, and a quarter second later the slug hammered the far side of the boulder, throwing rock slivers in every direction.

Longarm snaked the Winchester over the top of the boulder, aiming at the place where he'd seen the flash, and emptied the gun. The reports flatted out across the canyon, echoing. The empty cartridge casings clinked to the rocks over Longarm's right shoulder.

Upstream, a man grunted. There was the clatter of a dropped rifle. A man bounded out away from a tree stump and ran stumbling into the stream where, a few yards from shore, he dropped to his knees, clutching his belly. He sagged forward until he was on all fours, then slowly fell to his far shoulder, and lay still, the water gurgling and flashing up against him.

Knowing he had an empty rifle and that his gun flashes had given away his position, Longarm bolted out from behind the boulder and into a cleft amongst more boulders at the base of the ridge. He pressed his back into a corner, then eased himself down to his butt, breathing hard, slipping fresh cartridges from the loops on his belt, and feeding them through the loading gate of his hot, smoking rifle.

When he'd fed the Winchester nine rounds, he levered one into the chamber and sank back against the boulders, holding the rifle straight up and down in his right hand, stock resting against the ground. He waited.

Gradually, his breathing slowed. So did the blood washing through his ears.

When he could hear again clearly, he heard nothing but the stream for a long time.

Then a whinny rose from the direction of the corral.

There was the creak of the corral gate opening.

Longarm's heart twisted. They were getting the horses!

He bolted out from his hiding place and ran across the creek, knowing his splashing would give him away, but without the horses, he and the girl would be stranded here. He pushed through the trees and brush, hearing the thuds of galloping hooves. A mule brayed, and a horse whinnied.

Longarm gritted his teeth and pumped his knees as he ran. But he wasn't fifty yards from the stable before he saw it was too late. Two riders were hazing the horses off across the clearing, in the direction of where the main trail curved in. One rider whooped and hollered. The other fired a pistol into the air over the galloping herd.

Longarm dropped to a knee and raised his rifle.

A gun flashed from the nearest rider's jostling, silver-limned shadow. The slug tore into the ground two feet to Longarm's left.

Longarm triggered his rifle once, twice, three times. The rider cursed. Longarm lost the man in the darkness for a few seconds, then saw his horse drag him off across the clearing toward the main trail. He was grunting and groaning as he hoisted his back off the ground, trying to free his boot from its stirrup. Then he disappeared in the far trees and thick, dark night.

With Longarm's stock.

A gun barked near the cabin, setting Longarm's heart to racing once more.

He ran.

Chapter 16

Longarm was thirty yards from the cabin's front door when he saw Jo standing outside, facing slightly away from him. In her right hand, she held the peach-gripped pistol that Longarm had taken off one of the first three gang members he'd killed in the mountains.

She was aiming the gun slightly out away from her, at a man kneeling about ten yards from her. The man was crouched slightly, hands clamped over his belly. His hat was off, and his close-cropped, coal-black hair glistened in the starlight. A pistol lay on the ground before him, near his hat. He lifted his head toward Longarm, and the lawman saw the thick mustache that curved down over the man's wide knife slash of a mouth.

"Bitch killed me," he told Longarm without passion, as though he were imparting the time of day. He gurgled deep in his throat, and then he pitched forward against the ground, shoulders quivering slightly.

Jo lowered the pistol in her hand and brought her other hand to her mouth.

Longarm continued forward past Jo and crouched to pick up the dead man's pistol. He kicked the body over and pulled another pistol from a shoulder holster under the man's short wolf coat.

"I heard him out here," Jo said thinly, trying to keep her emotions in check as she stared down at the man she'd killed. "Just before they took the horses. I came out. I guess I surprised him."

"Better him than you."

Longarm shoved both spare pistols behind his cartridge belt, and snaked his arm around Jo's shoulders. He gave her a gentle squeeze and stared off across the clearing toward where the two riders and the horses and mules had disappeared. Vaguely, he could still hear the fleeing mounts' thudding hooves and cursed silently.

"I . . . never shot anyone before." She looked up at Longarm, her jaws firm. "Wasn't all that hard."

Longarm gave her another gentle squeeze. "Best get on inside. They'll be back."

She turned and walked into the cabin. Longarm followed her inside, leaving the door open so he could hear what was happening outside, and set both pistols on the table. He turned the lamp half up, spreading a dull, buttery glow about six feet out from the table.

Jo sagged silently into a chair on the table's opposite side, and Longarm went over to the range from which he picked up the coffeepot. He brought it over to the table and filled both their cups.

To each he added some Maryland rye. "Drink that. Settle your nerves."

"Thanks." She picked up the cup in both hands and brought it slowly to her lips.

Longarm returned the pot to the range, picked up his own cup, and carried it over to the open door, leaning a shoulder against the frame. He sipped the coffee and stared out at the night. He could see the dust still sifting in the wake of the galloping horses, but a heavy silence had again fallen.

Behind him, Jo swallowed, drew a breath, asked quietly. "How many are left?"

"I got three more. You got one. I'm thinking that leaves three or four, if I counted right."

"We're upping our odds."

Longarm nodded. "They got the horses, though. Now we have no choice but to stick it out here."

"See if they come back."

"They'll come. I was wrong before, but I'm right about this. This is a game for those fellas. They want vengeance, but mostly they want the hunt. You'd think that every time I killed one, the others would think twice about making another play."

Longarm shook his head and sipped his coffee. "That ain't how it is. They're like wolves. They'll keep comin' even when they're outnumbered. Even though there's nothing here for 'em but prey. No money or hope of money. Just prey."

Jo stared at him and shook her head. "I don't understand."

"Robbing banks and stagecoaches probably got old. Dull." Longarm stared toward the main trail, now hearing a distant coyote's forlorn call. "Just wasn't the challenge this is. They're on the blood scent now. They know it's either us or them. They like it. They like it too much. Means one thing."

"What's that?"

"Like rabid wolves, they need to be put down fast."

Jo took another deep breath and let it out slow as she stared down at the pistol before her. "Yes. I'll help in any way I can."

"Maybe you won't have to." Longarm glanced at her. "Close and bar the door behind me."

Her eyes grew afraid. "Please, don't leave me again, Longarm."

Longarm set his cup and rifle on the table and kneeled down in front of her, setting a hand on her denim-clad leg. "I'll be right outside. Won't stray more than ten feet away. Be in hailing distance at all times. I'm just gonna sit out here on the bench where I can keep an eye and ear on things." He patted her leg, rose, and kissed her. "Keep the coffee hot, will ya?"

She nodded as he picked up his rifle and coffee and went outside. When she'd closed the door behind him, he listened until he heard the locking bar slide into place, then walked a few feet into the yard, rifle on his shoulder, steaming cup in his hand.

Except for the still-mewling coyote and an occasional breeze rustle, there was only silence. He went over and sat down on the bench, and he was still there, several hours and cups of coffee later, when the sun smeared a pearl wash behind the eastern ridges. He lightly tapped on the door. Jo must have dozed off at the table, because it was a few second before he heard her chair scrape and her boots tap across the floor.

The locking bar scraped, and the door opened. "I must have nodded off."

A rifle cracked in the clearing behind Longarm. The slug hammered into the door to Longarm's left and only inches from Jo, who screamed, eyes widening and lower jaw dropping. Longarm threw himself forward and into the girl.

They hit the floor together hard, and as several more rifles barked, the slugs hammering the door and the cabin's front wall, flinging splinters, Longarm twisted around and kicked the door closed.

More slugs hammered it from the other side, making it jerk in its frame. Guns popped from at least two other directions, bullets thumping into the rear and north walls. A shutter over one of the cabin's two rear windows blew open.

Jo said, "Oh!" and turned to it, her hair flying.

"Stay down."

Rising to a crouch, Longarm ran over to the window over the bed they'd made love in, used his rifle to close it as another slug tore into it, with a sound like a thunderclap, and latched it with his other hand. He pressed his back to the wall and looked around.

Jo was on the floor, belly down, chin lifted, pressing her hands to her ears. Her eyes were bright in the dim lamplight as she stared at Longarm.

He looked around the room, the cabin shaking as three gunmen hammered the place with lead—one from the front, one from the direction of the stable, the other from the rear.

"We're all right," he told Jo above the gun bursts and the hammering thuds of the bullets. "These walls are stout."

The last word was no sooner out of his mouth before a bullet split the chinking from two logs in the front wall, and flung it across the table, making the lamp chimney ring. It left a gap about two inches wide. Whoever was shooting from that direction was a good shot—he sent another slug hurling cleanly between the logs to screech across the cabin, then spang off the iron range about two feet to Jo's right.

"Over here!" Longarm ran over, grabbed her arm, jerked her up, and half dragged her over to the cot. She dropped onto it and pressed her back to the wall. "Stay here and whatever you do, keep your head away from the windows."

"Don't worry!" she shouted above the din, again covering her ears.

Longarm ran across the room, pressed his shoulder against the front wall, and snugged a cheek against the shutter over the window right of the door. He peered through a crack but he couldn't see anything.

The pearl wash was lightening gradually, but it was too dark to see much except for the steady burnt orange flares of the shooter's gun. He was hunkered down beneath a low knoll about fifty yards in front of the cabin.

Longarm pulled his head away, pressed his back against the wall, felt the logs shudder against the fusillade. He squeezed the Winchester in his hands, waited until the shooting gradually died as the shooters emptied their guns. They each must have been packing several weapons, as the firing didn't stop altogether until after they'd been shooting for three or four minutes.

When a heavy silence followed, punctuated by the whoops and yells of the ambushers, Longarm jerked the front shutter open, snaked his rifle outside, and fired two quick rounds where he'd seen the stab of the gun flames.

In the milky morning light, he watched his bullets kick up dust. One gave a spanging whistle as it ricocheted, evoking a mocking whoop from the man hunkered there. As the man cackled loudly, Longarm slammed the shutter closed and pressed his back against the wall once more.

No point in returning fire until the sun rose a little higher, so he could get a better fix on what he was shooting at. He'd let them deplete their own ammo stores. His biggest worry was that they might try to burn him out. He'd have to return fire every now and then to make sure they didn't dare a sprint to the cabin.

Otherwise, he'd bide his time, wait for the light to grow.

He waited a few minutes, gritting his teeth with quiet fury as the bullets continued to hammer the cabin though more sporadically than before. They must have figured out his plan and realized, even in their kill frenzy, that they were playing into his hands. He pushed away from the wall and, glancing at Jo, who was hunkered belly down on the bed now, moved over to the window in the wall facing the stable.

A couple of slugs hammered that wall as he reached out to flip open the shutter's latch, then pushed the shutter away from the frame with his rifle barrel. He waited for one more shot to hammer the wall from that direction, then snaked his rifle out the window.

It was light enough now that he could see smoke wafting from between two lower corral poles, even saw a vague figure hunkered there and raising his rifle's barrel as he cocked the weapon.

Longarm aimed hastily and fired three shots, the ejected casings clicking around his boots, and grinned as he heard the shooter curse and watched him throw himself over the stock trough and out of sight.

The man out front of the cabin shouted, "You all right over there, Crowfoot?"

"Got a chunk o' wood in my eye!" Crowfoot shouted. Then, louder: "You son of a bitch in there!" Longarm latched the shutter as two slugs hammered it furiously.

Again, Longarm grinned. As all three shooters continued to send slugs careening into the walls around him, the lawman made his way across the cabin to the window just behind the eating table. A bullet hammered it, and then he flipped the latch and nudged the shutter open with his rifle barrel.

He edged a look around the frame. There was enough light now that he could see the shooter hunkered down behind a deadfall log, aiming a rifle toward the cabin.

Longarm jerked his head back as the rifle stabbed smoke and flames from its maw, the slug chewing into the frame exactly where the lawman's head had just been. Cocking the Winchester, he poked the rifle out the window and squeezed the trigger. He watched the slug blow chunks of wood from the top of the log a quarter second after the man had pulled his head down behind it.

He ejected the spent shell and narrowed his eyes as he continued staring out the window. About ten feet behind the shooter, between the log and the creek, the shooter had built a small fire. Several dead branches lay in the fire, half in and half out of it.

"Goddamnit."

"What is it?" Jo asked from the bed, lifting her head to peer up between her elbows.

Longarm pressed his cheek against the Winchester's stock, aiming. He waited. The crown of the shooter's hat appeared. Longarm waited another moment, and when he saw the shooter's eyes beneath his hat brim, he squeezed the trigger.

The man pulled his head back down behind the log.

Longarm's slug blew his hat off and set it sailing into the fire.

"You son of a bitch!" the man cried, his voice muffled by the log.

Longarm hammered the log with three more angry rounds, then pulled his head back away from the window and closed and latched the shutter.

Jo was still staring at him. "What is it, Longarm? What'd you see out there?"

"Oh, nothin'." Longarm waited, pensive, running his thumb along his Winchester's breech. "They're gonna try to burn us out. That's all."

Chapter 17

"Send that blond-headed poontang out here, lawdog, and save yourself! You keep her in there, you're *both* gonna die!"

The shouted threat had come from behind the low knoll at the front of the cabin.

Jo gasped.

Longarm opened the shutter over the front window right of the door. "You want her?" he shouted.

Jo gasped again.

"Here she is, you son of a bitch!"

He triggered three shots at the knoll, behind which the shooter there dropped just in time to avoid the hot lead blowing up dirt and grass clumps. Longarm slammed the shutter and latched it. A half second later, the three shooters opened up, hammering the cabin once more until dust sifted from the rafters.

Longarm dashed over to the window facing the corral, opened it, and clipped off two shots, missing Crowfoot again by a hair but setting him to squawking. Longarm cursed and slammed the shutter. He wanted to get the trio pared down. No way he and Jo were holding out for much longer . . .

The man shooting from the front paused to give a rebel yell. Longarm pressed his back against the wall, frowning as he slipped fresh cartridges through his Winchester's loading door. Had the yell been a signal?

He slipped one more shell through the loading gate, then headed over to the window behind the table, nudged it open with his rifle barrel. At the moment, no shots were being triggered from back there. He nudged a look toward the log behind which the west-side shooter had been firing.

Nothing—no movement except the fire whose light was fading now as the sun continued edging closer toward the eastern horizon, filling the canyon with a murky, pale glow.

Longarm ran across the cabin toward the window at the far end. Running footsteps sounded on the other side of the shutter, growing louder. Longarm unlatched the shutter, flipped it open, poked his rifle out the window, pressed his cheek against the stock, and grinned.

A man stopped dead in his tracks about twenty feet from the cabin, his eyes snapping wide in shock. On his head was a battered brown Stetson with a hole through its crown. He was unshaven, long-haired, with a small blue cross tattooed on the nub of his right, leathery cheek.

With his right hand he gripped a burning branch. His carbine was in his left. Obviously, he'd been making a run for the cabin, intending to toss the burning branch onto the roof.

Longarm's grin widened. The man's eyes acquired a look of bald horror. He screamed and cocked his throwing arm, bringing the branch back behind his shoulder, cocking it to throw.

Longarm's Winchester roared. The slug tore through the middle of the man's chest, between the flaps of his red-striped blanket coat. The man dropped his rifle. Both hands fell to his sides as he stumbled straight backward and fell hard on his back, tossing the branch in the air.

The torch landed on his chest. The man screamed and flopped his arms and legs as though trying to shuck the branch away from him. After a few seconds, it slithered down his side to the ground but not before flames were leaping up from his burning shirt and coat and he was screaming like a schoolgirl who'd just found a coiled diamondback in the privy.

The other ambushers had stopped shooting. All Longarm could hear at the moment was the crackling of the flames now edging up and down the length of the dying man's flopping body.

A voice yelled from the front, "You're gonna pay for that, lawdog."

Longarm sensed someone behind him. He turned,

saw Jo crouched beside him, staring out the window. She slid her eyes from the burning man to Longarm. Her green eyes looked more hopeful than horrified.

Longarm closed and latched the shutter. He strode to the front window, peeled the shutter back, and pressed his back against the wall beside it. "Why don't you come in here and make me pay? Or pull out now while you still can," he shouted. "How many did you start out with? How many you down to?" Fury burned bright in the lawman's eyes. "Come on, you lame-assed son of a bitch. You wanna dance—let's dance!"

Longarm jerked his rifle out the window, took aim at the pale oval of the man's face beneath the curled brim of his piss-yellow Stetson, and fired three shots. The gunman gave a mocking whoop as he pulled his head down, and Longarm's bullets blew up dust where the killer's face with its devilish, close-set eyes had just been.

Longarm pulled the Winchester out of the window and pivoted to the window's other side, leaving the shutter open.

"Jo, I'm gonna need your help."

She was kneeling in a corner of the room, holding her pistol in both hands against one thigh. Her eyes were bright as she nodded and hardened her jaws. "You got it."

"We're gonna get this thing over with, goddamnit," Longarm said, jerking his head toward the open shutter. "Come over here but stay clear of the window."

When she was standing on the other side of the

window from him, holding her pistol up against her breasts and looking at him anxiously, he said, "One down. Two to go."

She swallowed, gave her chin a little, tense dip. "That's right." She paused, gazing at him. "What're you gonna do, Longarm?"

Both men had started shooting again, the slugs plunking into the window frame near Longarm and Jo, the others peppering the northern wall. The shooters were cackling and yowling like demented banshees, trying their hardest to add terror to their fusillade.

"I want you to very carefully trigger shots from this window while I trigger shots from the other one. When we have both men down behind their covers, I'm jumping out that window over there and making a beeline for the corral."

"What about the man in front?"

"You'll hold him down with the pistol. Don't worry about hitting him. Just keep his head down."

"But I only have six shots."

"That's all you'll need. When I've beefed the killer in the corral, I'm gonna circle around behind the other man and beef him, too."

Jo just stared at him, eyes wide as wheel hubs.

"You know how to shoot that thing, right?" Longarm asked her hopefully.

"Yes. I've fired a pistol before."

Longarm chuffed, remembering the hotel in Snow Mound. "Yeah, I remember." He gave her an encouraging wink. "Good enough." He started to edge away from the front window. "When I give the word, start shootin'."

Longarm slipped over to the north window. A shot battered the shutter. He jerked it open, waited for one more shot from the corral, then glanced at Jo. "Wait for a break, then start shooting. Keep his head down but if you see his rifle, pull your head back out of the way!"

"Be careful, Longarm!"

Longarm poked his rifle out the window and fired three rounds, blowing up dust and horseshit around the stock trough behind which the man in the corral was hunkered, causing him to pull his own head down out of sight. Continuing to shoot, Longarm dropped one leg out the window, then the other, and hearing Jo open up on the man in the front, started running as fast as he could while triggering the Winchester from his hip.

He was ten feet from the trough when his rifle clicked on an empty chamber. The shooter bolted up from behind it, mouth wide as he gave a victorious bellow, eyes spitting fire. He jerked his rifle up just as Longarm snaked his hand across his belly to grab his Colt, bringing it up in a blur, crouching, and firing.

The shooter did a weirdly graceful little pirouette as he fired his Henry repeater straight down, blowing a hole through his own left foot, then raising both arms as though to click his thumbs in mariachi rhythms before falling facedown in a cloud of wafting dust. Blood pooled quickly beneath his bullet-riddled chest.

Behind Longarm, Jo screamed. Even muffled by the cabin walls, it bespoke unbridled terror.

Longarm spun, crouching over his six-shooter extended straight out from his belly. He held fire when he saw the third and sole surviving killer throw himself through the cabin door with a loud roar of breaking wood and flying hinges. Again, Jo screamed.

The killer laughed loudly.

Longarm ran, scissoring his arms and legs, terror clawing at him. Jo had likely fired all six of her pistol shots . . .

The screech of shattering glass emanated from the gaping cabin door. The man yowled.

"*Ahhh* . . . no! No, no, *noooo!*"

Longarm stopped when he saw a ball of fire come flying out of the cabin. The burning ball had arms and legs and even a piss-yellow hat. Longarm could smell the burning leather and hair. The man ran shamblingly about twenty feet out from the cabin and, still yelling and burning, swung his rifle toward Longarm, who crouched and capped the last three shells in his Colt.

Bam-bam-bam!

The killer spun like a giant, burning top, then dropped to his knees. Longarm could smell the burning flesh. Jo appeared in the cabin's open doorway.

"Oh, God!" she cried, clapping a hand to her mouth.

"The lamp?" Longarm asked.

She nodded.

"You did damn good, gir—"

A loud pop cut him off. Jo gasped.

"Get back inside!" Longarm shouted, then ran to the cabin. He shoved the girl inside, pulled her down beside him, and they both hunkered against the front wall.

More explosions sounded like a string of Mexican firecrackers detonating at a Cinco de Mayo parade.

"Are there more gunmen?" Jo cried, covering her ears and staring worriedly up at Longarm.

"Nah." Longarm shook his head, grinning. "That's just the shells in his cartridge belt goin' off!"

There were a few more sporadic explosions, then silence. Longarm placed two fingers under the girl's chin and tipped her head back, smiling. "It's over," he said. "And you did damn good, Jo."

Her eyes brightened. She lowered her hands from her ears and threw her arms and body around Longarm with such passion that he fell over his heels and hit the shack's floor on his back. "I'm not doomed," she cried. "I'm not doomed after all!"

Longarm laughed.

She rammed her breasts tight against his chest as she mashed her hungry lips against his and snaked her tongue into his mouth, groaning like a bobcat with the springtime craze.

He and the girl stayed down there a long time before retiring to the bed.

Two weeks later, the narrow gauge pulled into Denver's Union Station, which was bustling with itinerant cowhands and drummers even at midnight on a Tuesday.

His shoulders bowing beneath the weight of all

his gear, Longarm stepped off the train with a tired groan, weary from the long trek out of the hills with Jo Pritchard. He'd seen the girl back to her town and waiting family.

She wouldn't be returning to the bank or her former boss, Mr. Cable, however. She thought she might teach school, as Pinecone had been looking for a teacher for quite some time.

Now, remembering the slow journey with the doomed young woman from Pinecone, the long nights of tender, passionate frolic around crackling campfires, he made his way through the big sandstone hulk of Union Station and rented a hansom cab on Wynkoop Street. A half hour later, he paid the driver, stepped down from the cab, and made his way up the brick walk of his rented digs on the poor side of Cherry Creek.

Oh, Lordy—his bed was going to feel good!

He tramped up the outside stairs of his second-story flat in the neat, white-frame rooming house and froze in his boots. He stared down past the knob and lock plate of the green-painted pine door, his tired heart picking up a reluctant warning rhythm in his chest.

The half length of stove match he'd wedged between the door and the frame had fallen to the sill. It lay there on the painted oak, its red sulfur tip and ragged opposite end staring up at him in mute testament to surefire danger.

Longarm studied the door before narrowing a hopeful eye. "Cynthia . . . ?"

Watch for

LONGARM AND THE RANGE WAR

the 398th novel in the exciting LONGARM
series from Jove

Coming in January!

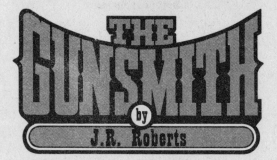